L. J. WESTON

CHARLIE
BOY

A FARM BOY RIDES TO WAR

L. J. WESTON

CHARLIE BOY

A FARM BOY RIDES TO WAR

MEREO
Cirencester

Published by Mereo

Mereo is an imprint of Memoirs Publishing

1A The Market Place Cirencester Gloucestershire GL7 2PR
info@memoirsbooks.co.uk | www.memoirspublishing.com

Charlie Boy

ISBN: 978-1-86151-115-7

Chapter One

It was a spring morning in 1912, and the daffodils were out in the garden and the crocuses in their late stages of bloom. There was a bang on the door of the farmhouse, and I opened it to find the postman holding out a very official-looking letter. It had my name on it.

"Is your mum or dad in?" said the postman.

"It's for me" I said. "I'm Charlie Carson."

"Sign here then."

What could it be? I wondered whether it was from the police, a summons perhaps, and they had put my name on the letter instead of that of Albert, my brother, known to us all as Bert. He was always getting into trouble. It was Bert who had jumped off the top of the bus when we went for a day out last week. The conductor had shouted out, "That's the last time you'll jump off the top of my bus. I know where you live. I'm going to report you to the police." Bert just said, "He doesn't know where we live, he's bluffing".

I don't know why Bert was so impatient when we reached the bus stop, to jump off the top of the bus instead of going down the stairs. His twin Fred kept telling him

"You'll break your bloody legs one of these days, you mad fool!"

I ran upstairs with the letter and closed the door. I ripped the letter open and was amazed to read that I had been selected to run in the Olympic Games. The letter really was for me. The games were the fifth Olympic Games, to be held that summer, and I was asked to reply immediately and say whether I would like to take part.

I was very excited, as the games were to take place in Stockholm, and I had never been abroad. No one we knew went abroad, except those who went to fight, like Dad, who had been sent to South Africa in 1899 to fight in the Boer War. I had been only two years old when he left, and Mum had had to bring up us three young children on her own, which was very difficult for her. Fred and Bert had been only five and Dad hadn't returned home until the war was over in 1902.

I went downstairs with the letter and showed it to Mum, who was the only one in the house, Dad, Fred and Bert having all gone to work. Mum was so pleased that she began pacing up and down the kitchen with excitement.

"Wait till Dad gets home, won't he be surprised" she said. "He always said you wouldn't amount to much, that all you wanted to do was ride that horse of yours. Just wait till he gets home!"

★ ★ ★

It was six o'clock in the evening and I had put Bessie, my

mare, in the stable for the night. It wasn't really a stable, though we all called it that, it was more like a big shed. I went into the house with muddy boots on as usual and Mum yelled out "Take that mud outside!"

I sat down on the back doorstep and kicked off my boots and banged them against the side of the house to get most of the mud off. Then I got some newspaper and stood them on the paper inside the back door.

"Shut that back door, you're letting all the heat out!" Mum yelled. "And you can put some more coal on the fire while you're at it."

I did what Mum told me and there was a nice blazing fire when Dad, Fred and Bert arrived home at 6.30 pm. They all worked together on the farm just outside the gate at the bottom of the garden, growing vegetables and flowers which they sold in the marketplace in town. I looked after the chickens and geese in the yard. It was my job to collect the eggs in the morning, and these were sold in the market after Mum had taken out what she needed for the family.

I didn't say anything about the letter until everyone had finished their tea. Mum glanced at me and said, "Well go on then, tell Dad about the letter."

"What letter?" Dad said. "Have you got a letter? Who's written to you? You're too young for the Army. Give it here."

I gave Dad the letter and everyone sat in silence around the table while Dad read it.

"Well well well" said Dad. "Fancy that, so you are good

at something then." Fred and Bert both shouted together "Go on Dad, tell us what it says."

"It seems the Olympic Committee want Charlie here to run in the games" said Dad.

Fred and Bert jumped up excitedly and both slapped me on the back. "Well done Charlie boy, you show 'em!" said Fred. "You show 'em you can run like a deer. No one will be able to catch you, Charlie boy!"

Bert said "You'll win a gold medal. Gold! That'll be worth a lot of money. It'll help towards buying the cows we've always wanted so we can start a real farm."

I was so excited that night that I couldn't go to sleep. I could see myself running like a hare round that big track with everyone cheering me on. "Run Charlie, run!" they were all shouting.

I woke with a start, hearing Bert's voice. "I'll kill that bloody cockerel! Look at the clock, it 's only just gone half past bloody four."

There was only a faint glimmer of light in the yard. Bert always got so bad tempered when he was woken from a deep sleep, and he was down the stairs in a flash. I watched from the window and I could see him chasing the cockerel round the yard with a chopper.

Dad woke up and yelled out of the window, "Put that chopper down. Don't you harm a feather on that bird's head, or I'll swing for you!"

Bert shouted back, "You kill him or I bloody well will!"

We were all a bit bleary-eyed at the breakfast table, but this was pretty normal for us. When Bert had finished his breakfast he went out into the yard, and when Dad wasn't looking he kicked the cockerel up the backside, which made it almost take off, clucking like mad. Bert went out of the gate, followed by Fred, but Dad stayed back talking to Mum, who was already hanging out the washing.

I don't know what was being said, but Mum looked really upset. When I saw Dad leave the yard through the gate I quickly ran up to her and asked her what Dad had said to her to make her look so unhappy. She was nearly in tears.

"What's up? What did Dad say to you?" I asked her.

Picking up her apron and blowing her nose on the corner of it, she said, "I'm sorry son."

"Sorry for what, Mum?"

"Dad can't afford to let you go to the Olympics. He has set his heart on buying some cows, and there won't be money for both. We just don't have the money son, not for the fare and your keep in Stockholm as well."

I was quite shocked. I hadn't thought of the cost of running in the Olympics. Immediately I knew that the idea of ever running abroad was out of the question.

I was heartbroken. I started to kick at the ground, then at the fence, tears welling up in my eyes. I ran to the barn and got Bessie, my little brown mare, out and rode her bareback across the field. I rode out into the lane and crossed into Mr Barney's field. I galloped across his field and then into the next, and finally I threw myself to the ground under a giant oak. I sobbed and sobbed until I could cry no more.

I made a vow never to go back to the athletics club. All that training, every week – for what? I'll join the army, I thought to myself, that's what I'll do. I *will* go abroad, not this year, but next, I *will* see the world!

★ ★ ★

As the days passed by I still felt listless and unhappy, but I tried to knuckle down to the chores as I knew that thinking about the army too much was only making me feel more depressed. I wouldn't be fifteen until November that year. There was only one way to get in; I would have to lie about my age, and in the meantime I would build up my muscles and get myself fit, and in good shape.

On the morning of April 16th I was woken from my sleep by Dad yelling up to me from the bottom of the stairs.

"Get up Charlie and get dressed and go down to the corner shop for me and get me a newspaper, here's threepence. Hurry up!"

"What's up? You normally have the late paper."

"You'll never guess what's happened" said Dad. "The *Titanic* has sunk. Go on, get me a newspaper, you can have your breakfast when you come back."

I ran down the lane across the field and across the village green. There was quite a crowd around the little corner shop with people just standing there with their heads in the newspaper.

'TITANIC DISASTER' it said on the front of the

paper. Only a few days earlier we had been reading about her departure on her maiden voyage from Southampton, and now that glorious ship had sunk after hitting an iceberg. Some passengers had been rescued by another ship, but many had died. I ran home with the newspaper and gave it to Dad, who was waiting at the gate.

"Maiden voyage as well" he said. "Looks like it sank early yesterday morning. To think of all those people drowning in that icy water."

We all sat down at the kitchen table until almost lunch time, with Dad reading the paper out loud to all of us. "Well mother" he finally said. "We might as well have something to eat and get out on the land, there's nothing we can do about those poor unfortunate souls."

The *Titanic* disaster was the topic of conversation everywhere for weeks. No one seemed to talk about anything else.

As life was getting back to normal that summer, both Fred and Bert enlisted in the army. They were now eighteen years old, Fred being the elder by about half an hour - he never let Bert forget that he was the eldest son. He would boss Bert about so much you would have thought that he was years older.

Dad said to me, "You know you'll have to come and work on the farm with me now. Mum will have to look after the chickens and the geese in the yard and do your chores."

He was quite upset that the twins would be going away, as he had relied on them so much. He went out into the yard and leaned over the gate, puffing on his pipe and staring out across the fields.

The time went by very quickly, and before we knew it Fred and Bert were packing their bags ready to leave and join their regiment.

"We're off now then, Dad" said Fred. Dad hugged them both in turn, holding them tightly to his chest. It was the first time I can remember ever seeing him hug them.

They went into the kitchen and hugged Mum, who was crying hysterically. "My boys, my boys!" she sobbed. "Look after one another and don't go volunteering for anything dangerous. Come back safely!"

"Bye Charlie" said Bert. They both punched me playfully on the arms. "Your turn will come soon enough."

Yes, I thought to myself, I'll be in the army next year.

As they were leaving, Bert put his head round the door and said "If you get a chance, and accidentally on purpose kill that bloody cockerel, I'll be bloody grateful. I don't want it here when I get back – understood? Bye Charlie" Bert winked at me as he waved goodbye.

I knew I would feel lonely without Fred and Bert. They had only just gone, and I was already missing them.

I went upstairs and lay on my bed. I looked around the room and saw the twins' empty beds. Mum had just folded the blankets up. She had already taken off the sheets and they had been washed and were now hanging on the line to dry. She had folded the quilts and had put them on top of the beds. We called them quilts, but they were just made from squares cut out from old overcoats which Mum had sewn together to make a big envelope, which she had stuffed with clean rags and sewn up. But they were snug and warm and we were glad of them on cold winter nights.

I must have fallen asleep. I only came to when I heard Dad yelling out "Charlie, Charlie, are you up there? Get yourself down here, there's work to be done. The cabbages need to be cut and sacked."

I jumped off the bed and ran downstairs. Mum was ironing the sheets from the two beds, so I knew I had slept for some time.

"Dad has gone out in the field, you had better have your tea when you have helped him bring in the cabbages" she said. "There's no use bending on a full stomach. Well off you go, and don't forget to give Bessie some new straw before you come back in."

I worked alongside Dad until it was almost dark. He wanted to cut all the cabbages and clear the whole field so that he could get it ready for replanting. We put the cabbages in sacks at the end of each row, but when it was time to lift the sacks onto the cart I nearly fell over under the weight. Although I was big for my age, I struggled with them.

"All right Charlie, leave that to me" said Dad. "You go and get Bessie, we'll need her, we'll hitch her to the cart. I can't pull the cart without your brothers, she'll have to earn her keep now."

By the time I sat down for tea I was too exhausted to eat. "Come on son eat up, or you'll be no use to me tomorrow" Dad went on.

Tomorrow, tomorrow! The way I was feeling I didn't think I would be able to move a muscle ever again, let alone tomorrow.

Chapter Two

Two weeks went by, and my chores didn't get any lighter. The third week after Fred and Bert had left, a fair arrived down on the green. Dad said that if we worked hard and finished our chores by Friday, I could have the whole of the weekend off.

Saturday morning came at last. I didn't get up until around nine o'clock. Somehow or other I didn't hear the cockerel crowing earlier; maybe I was in such a deep sleep, or maybe he had snuffed it, because if he was up, normally, everyone was up.

"What happened to the cockerel this morning?" I said to Mum.

"Oh Dad took him off early in the cart, he knew you were very tired, he'll be back shortly."

Dad came in when I was finishing my breakfast and asked me what I was going to do on my weekend off.

"I don't know yet, maybe I'll go down to the fair on the green later on" I said.

"Well don't go far this morning in case I need you" he said.

"So much for my weekend off" I said to Mum.

"Well you know Dad has lots to do" she replied. "I'll help him pick the gooseberries this afternoon. I know you hate the thorns."

"Yes, it's a pity they don't grow on the ground like strawberries" I said.

I took myself off down the lane straight after lunch, and soon ran into Harry Jenkins, who was coming out of Barney's field. Harry and I had been best mates up until he got into a bit of trouble stealing eggs from the Thomas' farm half a mile away. Dad found out about it from local gossip and said I wasn't to hang around with him. "He'll be pinching our eggs next" Dad said. "You keep away from the likes of him."

Poor Harry, it wasn't entirely his fault that he stole. His dad was a bit of a drunk and there never seemed to be enough money for his mother to buy food. She was a dear lady and would always give me something to eat when I went over to their house, in spite of them having hardly anything for themselves.

"Where you going Charlie?" he asked.

"Oh, I'm just going down to the fair to see what's happening down there" I said. "That's after I've had a sleep in the hay. I'm still a bit tired from helping my Dad, its been hard since Fred and Bert left, I've hardly stopped working."

"Yeah, I was wondering what you'd been up to all this time, not seeing you around."

"Where you going?" I asked.

"Same as you. I'm going to get some money this afternoon."

"Oh yeah? And how you gonna do that?"

"Well, I'm going to take on Big Joe the boxer. If you last three rounds they pay you three shillings."

"Don't be so bloody daft!" I said to him as I crashed out in a haystack on the edge of the field. "You won't last one round with a professional boxer. He'll beat you to a pulp."

"Well I reckon I can go three rounds with him if I keep out of his way. I'll dance around him, ducking and diving - you only have to be standing up at the end of the three rounds."

"What are you going to do with the money if you manage to be standing on your feet after three rounds?"

"I'll give Mum one shilling and the other two shillings I want to spend on an airgun."

"What do you want with an airgun?"

"I want to go rabbiting. Rabbits make a nice stew. You can come with me if you like."

"Surely its cheaper to make a snare" I said as I stretched out in the hay. "Maybe I'll come, maybe not. Let's see how you get on with this bloke Big Joe first." I stretched out. "I'm going to sleep for a while."

"OK" said Harry. "I'll stay with you, the fight's not till four o'clock."

At about three o'clock we got to our feet and carried on down the lane. When we turned the corner down the hill and walked through a line of trees we could hear the noise of the fair. There was music and kids shouting and screaming. We could see swings and merry-go-rounds and lots of tents, and we could smell toffee apples and candy floss being made.

"That big tent over there Charlie, that's where I'm heading." Harry pointed to a huge grey tent with red letters on it which read 'Boxing at 4 pm.' As we got closer we saw a sign which read, 'Step This Way. If You Can Go 3 Rounds With Big Joe You Win 3/-.'

Harry turned to me. "You coming in Charlie, to watch me box?"

"Yeah, I'll come in, but I think you better weigh this bloke up carefully first, to see how big and muscley he is before you go jumping into the ring with him."

There was a crowd of people already in the tent and more people were entering from both sides. The manager of the boxer was in the ring yelling out, "Who wants to take on Big Joe?"

Then Big Joe climbed into the ring in his shorts and dressing gown, waving his arms in the air and flexing his muscles. He was at least five foot eleven and heavily-built with a mean grin.

Harry shouted. "I'll fight him!" The ringmaster looked in our direction. "Was that you who shouted?" he said to me. "Yeah, it was me" I said. Harry looked at me in horror. "Charlie, what are you doing?" he said.

"I'm going to fight him."

"No you're not, if anyone stands a chance of beating this hulk it will be me."

I yelled out, "I'll go four rounds with him for four shillings!"

"Done!" the ringmaster shouted back, laughing. "Get yourself up here, son."

Harry was hopping mad, but I was determined. "Come on Harry" I said. "You can be my second, bring me the stool and that. We'll split the prize money."

"Yeah, if you win" said Harry dismissively.

"Well, I stand a better chance than you do, you've never boxed in your life before, as far as I know. Sure you've had fights, but never boxed. At least I've got a bit of experience, especially being around Fred and Bert."

I got in the ring, Harry close on my heels. Harry introduced himself as my second and got out of the ring. I tightened the belt round my trousers and a pair of gloves was handed to me.

Big Joe and I eyed one another as I waited in my corner for the bell to ring. The bell went and we touched gloves. Before I knew it, the big guy had landed me a punch on the chin and sent me sprawling across the canvas.

"Get him Charlie!" I could hear someone shouting. There seemed to be plenty of my pals dotted about the ringside. I got a glimpse of them now and then, but I didn't want to take my eyes off this guy for more than a fraction of a second. He was built like a bull and his punches were very heavy and sent me reeling this way and that. I tried to dance out of his way, but he landed me a blow on my right ear, and that made me really mad.

I knew I could go four rounds with this bloke if I could just land a few punches to his body. I was a bit taller than Harry at five foot six, but this guy had a longer reach than me and to have any chance of beating him I would have to get him to come down a bit nearer to my level. Then, if I got a chance, I would punch him hard in the solar plexus and then on the chin.

"Hit him in the guts!" someone yelled, and I thought to myself, that's exactly what I'm going to do if only I can get close enough. But still the blows were raining down on me and I fell backwards.

The bell rang just in time, as I could feel myself going down. I managed to get to my corner, where Harry sat me down and sponged my face, which was already bleeding. The bell rang and Harry pulled me to my feet saying "Go get him Charlie!"

Round Two went better. I shuffled towards the big guy, flinging punches at him, first a left and then a right, and I caught him off guard. I landed a punch to his gut with my left fist which made him double up, and when his head came down I landed a full upper-cut to his chin with my right fist. To my surprise he went down and stayed down to the count of six. I could see I had hurt him. After he got up he stayed back, guarding his face with his fists and only throwing short jabs into the air.

The bell went again and this time Harry was jumping about saying "You've got him Charlie! Just two more rounds, but get him in the next round, knock him out with a right and then a left hook."

Round Three. I've got to get him quickly, I kept saying to myself over and over, as I knew if I gave this big guy time to recover I would be finished. I tried to ward off his blows and managed successfully to duck and dive out of his way, then tried to find my way into his body to land a few heavy punches.

"Come on Charlie, get him!" someone shouted, and I knew that was what I had to do, but I had to wait and keep well out of the way of his left fist. He had an almighty punch and I didn't want to be on the receiving end of it a second time.

Then I got my chance. He lowered his left fist slightly and I threw a punch with my right which caught him under the ribs. Then I threw a left and he went down on the canvas. This time he stayed down for the count of ten. He struggled to his feet, but the fight was all over, and it was Harry who was lifting my arm in the air and calling me the champ.

My face felt as if it had been kicked by a horse. My right eye was swelling up and my nose was still bleeding. My vest was splattered with blood, and I had blood on my trousers. What would Mum say?

The fight manager came up to me and pressed four shillings into my hand, congratulating me on winning. "Well done" he said. "Perhaps you'd like to come and see me tomorrow, we may be able to sort something out for you in the boxing ring if you're interested in being a fighter." I didn't answer him.

"Well done" people were saying as I left the ring. The crowd surged forward and were patting me on the back. They seemed pleased that I had knocked the big fellow out.

Harry had followed me out of the tent. "Well done mate, well done" he said.

"Here" I said to Harry, holding out two shillings.

"No I couldn't take that mate, you earned every penny of it."

"A deal's a deal" I said to him, shoving the money into his hand.

"Thanks Charlie, you're a pal. Course, you do know you tired Big Joe out with your fancy footwork? Otherwise I would have had to scrape you off the canvas." He was grinning. "How about coming over to have a look at the horses? That's if you can make it that far."

"There's nothing wrong with my legs" I replied as we headed off towards the far end of the fair, where all the horses were tethered in a ring.

"You can't afford to buy a horse" I said to him.

"No, but I can still look. Maybe some day I'll come here and who knows, I might be able to pick out the best of the bunch and say "I'll have that stallion over there", and then I'll shove a fist full of money at the trader."

"Everyone can dream" I said. "Who knows, maybe you'll have the money some day Harry, you've got two bob towards it already, but make sure you get a bill of sale if you buy a horse at a fairground. Some of these horse traders get their horses funny ways."

"You mean they could be stolen?"

"Yes, that's exactly what I mean."

I stayed with Harry a little while looking over the horses, and you've never set eyes on a mangier-looking bunch.

"Well there's no great stallion here today Harry" I said. "I'm going home while I can still see."

"Yeah Charlie, you go home and get a bit of steak on that eye of yours, you've got a real shiner there."

When I reached home I decided to sneak round the back way to avoid Dad. The door to the parlour was open just a little way and I could see him in one of the armchairs, reading a newspaper. The parlour was the best room in the house and Mum used to keep it shut up most of the time. We kids weren't allowed in except on special occasions, that's if anyone came visiting, which wasn't very often. There was no one about, and I went through the hall and up the stairs as quickly and as quietly as I could to my room.

It still felt funny calling it 'my room'. It had always been known as 'Fred and Bert's room'; it had never been called 'Fred, Bert and Charlie's room'. I guess Mum and Dad got tired after they said 'Fred and Bert' and couldn't manage the Charlie part, or maybe I just didn't count.

I quickly went to the chest of drawers and got out one of Fred's shirts. I didn't have many shirts, and besides, Fred wouldn't be wanting his, or Bert for that matter, for some time. I stripped off my clothes and went into the bathroom. I got a bowl of water and plunged my face straight into it.

I must have had my face in the bowl for just a few seconds when I felt someone pushing my head down into the bowl. I started gasping for air and flailing my arms about. I managed to push myself up out of the bowl and then lashed out at whoever it was trying to drown me.

"OK, OK, it's only me" said Bert's voice. I looked up, but I couldn't see him properly as both my eyes were closing up, and I was having a hard job trying to see.

"What the bloody hell have you been up to?" said Bert. "Who did this to you? I'll bloody kill him!"

"What are you doing here?" I said, ignoring the question. I was so pleased to see Bert - or half-see him – that I flung my arms around him. I hadn't realized before just how much I loved and missed him and Fred, although they hadn't been away long.

"Where's Fred?" I asked. Then I heard voices downstairs - unmistakably Dad and Fred.

Bert said. "Yeah, we're both home on leave for a short while. So far we've been lucky, they've kept us pretty much together since we joined up. But look at your face! Has Dad seen you like this? What happened?"

"Oh, it's not what you think. The fair is down on the green and I entered into a fight in the ring. I was up against this big guy, but I knocked him down and won the fight."

Fred came into the bathroom then and looked at me and then at his shirt, which I had thrown over the bath. He was about to moan at me, but stopped.

"Christ! Look at your face!" he said.

"He's been in a fight" said Bert.

"Well I can see that."

"No, a proper fight, in a boxing ring."

"Blimey! How many rounds did you go and how much did you get at the end for it? You did get paid, didn't you?"

"I knocked the other guy out in three rounds, and I got four shillings" I said.

"Well you should have got ten shillings, the mess you're in. You're going to be pretty sore for the next couple of weeks. I'll go down the lane and see if I can get you some ice from somewhere to put on your eyes. You'd better lie down and get some rest."

Bert and Fred took me to the bedroom and then went downstairs. I could hear them talking to Mum and Dad. Bert came back upstairs and said, "I've told Mum and Dad what you've been up to and if I were you I would stay out of their way for a bit. They're not too pleased that you've been in the boxing ring. In fact Dad's raving mad. Here, put this on your eye, maybe it will help."

Bert handed me a piece of steak which he had got from the larder in the kitchen. I held the meat over one eye then the other, then my cheek, then my chin, wherever the pain was the worst. I lay down, and it wasn't long before I drifted off to sleep.

★ ★ ★

It was morning when I woke. This time the cockerel was right on cue. The sun was coming up and it looked as though it was going to be a nice day.

My face was still hurting, and when I looked into the mirror I could see how black and blue I was. My arms were aching and so was my chest. I felt as if I had been run over by old Barney's tractor.

I went downstairs to find Mum getting breakfast ready.

"I heard what happened" she said, barely able to look at me. "You'd better get some ointment on those cuts before they go septic. I suppose there's no use me asking you not to box, you never listen to what I say. But I will say this, boxing is not the answer to your frustration about the Olympics. Something else will come along to occupy your time, you'll see. That's if you can stay in one piece until then." She had tears in her eyes.

"I promise I won't fight again Mum, not in the ring and not anywhere else if I can help it."

This seemed to cheer her up a little. She made me some breakfast, all the while mumbling to herself about her boys who never listened to her. She then said, "Dad has already gone out with the boys this morning into the fields, so just take it easy, OK?"

"OK Mum" I said. "I think I'll go and take Bessie over the fields for some exercise today, she hasn't been out for a while. There's a nice pasture by Barney's field, I'll let her graze there afterwards."

I left the house after breakfast and was riding Bessie at a canter down the lane when I saw Harry running along with someone. They were darting round trees and behind bushes and they were clearly trying not to be seen. I slowed Bessie down to a walk and followed them at a safe distance, watching them from behind the trees, trying to see what was going on. I followed them to Harry's house and watched them go inside, after looking around to see no one was in sight.

I waited for some time before I tethered Bessie to the fence and banged on the door. No one came, so I banged again and shouted "Harry it's me, Charlie, are you in there?"

Harry opened the door just a little way. "Are you coming out?" I asked him

"No, I can't."

"Why, you got company?"

"No I'm alone." As he said that a noise came from his back room.

"Sounds like you've got company to me" I said.

"All right Charlie, come in."

"What's up?"

"It's a friend of mine, he's in trouble, the police are after him. he's just robbed a place and he wanted somewhere to stay."

I grabbed Harry by the collar and pulled him out of the house. "Don't be a bloody fool!" I said. "Do you want to get into trouble too? Get him out now, otherwise you'll be an accessory to his crime, and you know what that means."

"No Charlie, what does that mean?"

"It means you'll be charged with the offence along with him. Tell him to go now, out the back door, do it now!"

"OK, I'll tell him he can't stay here, but I don't think he has anywhere else to go."

"Well that's his problem."

"OK Charlie. I'll be back in a minute."

Harry closed the door on me and after a few minutes

he came back and opened the door wide and said "He's gone Charlie, out the back way over the fields."

"Never do that again!" I said to him.

"But he's a friend Charlie, I try to help my friends if I can."

"That's all very well, but you don't want to go to prison with him, do you?"

"Oh, I don't think it will come to that."

"Well I know different. Come on, let's take a walk."

We walked across the fields in the opposite direction to the one Harry's friend had taken.

"Let's sit down for a while" I said to him after we had gone some distance. "I'll tell you about one of my dad's ancestors who thought he was doing a favour for someone, a robber too, as it so happened. You ever heard of Dick Turpin, the highwayman?"

"Yeah, everybody's heard of him."

"Well a long time ago one of my dad's ancestors owned an inn near the Great Wood. He felt sorry for Dick Turpin and hid him in his cellar. He was being chased by the Sheriff's men and they were hot on his heels. They'd been chasing him all over the countryside. They found Turpin in the cellar and they arrested him and my dad's ancestor too, because they said he was aiding and abetting a criminal and a fugitive. My dad's ancestor landed up in Newgate Prison, and he was lucky that he only got a short sentence. The magistrate said it was because it was his first offence and he was normally of good character. He was warned that if it happened again he could be transported to one of the British Colonies, Virginia, that's in America. He would have done seven years. So you see, you're still breaking the law by helping a villain and you could be arrested too."

"Is that really true Charlie, that your family knew Dick Turpin?"

"Yeah, so I've been told. He was finally hanged in 1739 for horse stealing. It's a long time ago now, but the story is still passed down through my family, like a kind of warning I suppose, to keep us from breaking the law. Horse stealing still goes on today, that's why I told you to be careful if you buy a horse from the fair. You have to make sure that the person who's selling it to you is the rightful owner. I've only ever stolen one thing, borrowed it really, and that's from Dick Turpin, 'cos I took the name of his horse. I called my horse Bessie. His horse was called Black Bess."

"Wow, you really are well connected Charlie."

"That's not being well connected, you daft bugger. Having important friends is being well connected. Have you heard my dad say when a thing is black 'It's as black as Newgate's knocker'? Well that's about the knocker on the iron doors of Newgate Prison."

"Yeah, I've heard your dad say that loads of times. Once when you came in from the fields I heard him say, 'Charlie, your face is as black as Newgate's knocker'. He says it quite often about lots of different things, but I didn't know exactly what he meant."

"Well, that's where the saying comes from, way back

all those years ago. I don't suppose you knew that in the olden days men were hanged in public for stealing? Things are a lot better now, but you still better not go breaking the law."

"I didn't know people were hanged for just stealing, I thought you had to kill someone to be hanged! You know a lot about the law do you, Charlie?"

"No, but soon after Fred and Bert joined the army Dad asked me to take some papers to a man in London. I rode Bessie there and it took me ages to get there, it's quite a long way. Well, you've never seen such a commotion in all your life. There were people with carts everywhere. There were fancy carriages, much better than what you see round here. Open-top buses of course and some motor cars. There were ruffians in raggedy clothes, and women with placards marching up and down the streets demanding to have the right to vote. There were also men dressed in fine fancy clothes and women too, all rushing here and there. Poor Bessie had the fright of her life with all the yelling and banging going on around her, she reared up several times with carts going this way and that. I had a job to keep her out of harm's way.

"One horse pulling a coal cart reared up and it came down on to a handcart loaded with books, and they went everywhere. I got off Bessie and helped the young lad pick up the books, he was really grateful. Then after he left I found one of his books by the side of the road, it was all about law. I thought I'd catch the lad up and give it to him, but I couldn't get through the crowds. I've still got it and I read some of the pages now and then. I don't understand a lot of it, but some of it I can make out what they're on about."

"Is that where you got adding and betting from?"

"Aiding and abetting. Yeah, that's right. It's got lots of stuff like that in it, so don't go harbouring any criminals again. I was glad to get back home out of all that noise, back to the peace of the farm. It took Bessie a couple of days to settle down and get back to her old self."

"What did your mum and dad say about your fight?"

"Mum was really upset, but I made her a promise that I wouldn't box again."

"Yeah, your face was a real mess. She must have been upset seeing you like that. I've never seen you look so ugly." He peered at me. "But the swelling has gone down a bit round your eyes."

I grabbed Harry round the neck and pretended to throttle him.

"Well I'm going home, and don't forget what I told you" I said.

"OK Charlie."

It was late when I got home, and everyone was having their tea. Dad, Fred and Bert were all deep in conversation about the farm. Mum was busy in the kitchen, and she got me some tea.

"What do you think about having some cows on the farm right away Charlie?" Dad said. "With Fred and Bert away, I thought I might turn that field to the north and half the potato field into a pasture for some cows. While they're here we could get that area fenced off. It's going to be hard to manage all the vegetables in the future without Fred and Bert." We all agreed that it would be a good idea to turn part of the farm over to cows.

The next morning we were out on the farm by seven o'clock and hard at work digging the holes for the new fence posts, which Dad had arranged to be delivered by early afternoon. With all four of us digging, we were finished in plenty of time to get some of the posts in that day.

After three days the fence was up and we were ready for the cows. We needed a cow shed, but Dad said he would convert Bessie's shed into a big one for the cows and build a new stable for her, which I was very pleased and excited about. Although Dad never paid a lot of attention to Bessie, I think he was every bit as fond of her as I was.

Dad said he had bought twenty cows and one bull and they would be arriving the next day. The man bringing the cows was going to tell Dad all he needed to know about looking after them and caring for them and milking them, although much of the time they would be grazing on the very fertile and green grass of the north pasture.

Fred and Bert were just putting the finishing touches to the gate when we heard the cows coming up the lane. Dad had bought them from Mr Brown, who had a farm about two miles away. He was driving them gently along. Fred, Bert and I all went down the lane to meet him. His son Ben was following behind the cows with the bull, which was tied with a rope round his head and muzzle and was pulling hard on it. Ben had to use all his strength to keep the bull under control. He looked a big ferocious fellow and I thought I wouldn't get too near him. They were driven through the gate and into the field, and Ben released the rope from the bull's head and muzzle while Fred closed the gate securely behind them. Fred, Bert, Ben and I all sat on the fence watching. The bull now seemed quite happy mingling with the cows.

Dad took Mr Brown up to the house to pay him. "Well if these cows produce quickly there should be a nice herd by the time we're demobbed from the army" Fred said to Bert. "And we'll have a real farm to come home to."

When Dad returned with Mr Brown Mum came out too, and leaned over the fence to look the cows over. "I hope you don't think I'm going to milk these" she said. Dad laughed. "No" he said. "I plan to get hired help if Charlie and I can't manage."

Mr Brown started to talk to Dad about buying some horses from him.

"Yeah, I could put them into that empty field over there which is all overgrown" he said. "It would be nice to have horses. But cows will have to do for now. It'll be some way in the future before I can afford to buy any horses."

We said our goodbyes to the Browns, Dad closed the yard gate behind them and we all headed up the path to the house. I went to bed that night thinking about horses. If only we could breed horses, that would really be something exciting to look forward to. Horses were the love of my life.

I was so tired I drifted off to sleep in no time at all. It seemed I had only been asleep a short while when the cock crowed and it was time to get up. Fred and Bert were leaving that day, and they had already packed their bags again. This time they were talking about the possibility of going overseas. There was a lot of talk about Kaiser Bill, whoever he was, some royal bloke in Germany who was related to our royal family. Fred said he was causing a lot of trouble, but that's all he could tell us.

"Well, we're off then, Charlie" said Bert. "At least you look better now than you did when we got home. You look almost handsome. Not as handsome as me of course."

Bert gave me a bear hug, then Fred did the same. It was different this time. We all knew it would be a long time before we would all be together again.

I watched from the side window as Fred was saying goodbye to Mum and Dad. I couldn't see Bert from there, so I went to the back window and there he was chasing the cockerel around the yard, trying to give him a last kick before leaving, but he wasn't quick enough and the cockerel flew up over the fence into the cows' field, clucking like mad.

I watched as Bert came round from the back of the house and said his goodbyes to Mum and Dad. I kept watching as they waved before turning to go down the lane. I didn't know it at the time, but I would never see Bert alive again.

Chapter Three

As the weeks passed slowly and uneventfully by, Fred and Bert were never far from our minds. One morning when I had washed and dressed and had gone down to breakfast I could hear Dad in the parlour rustling the newspaper, and as I put my head round the door I saw him stuffing it under the cushion of the armchair. Why was he doing that, I wondered?

I went into the kitchen and Dad came in shortly after; we all had breakfast together. Dad sat in silence, I guess his thoughts were on whatever he had just been reading, while Mum's were with Fred and Bert, wondering when she would see them again.

Once Dad had left the house and Mum had got up to wash the dishes, I slipped into the parlour and fished the newspaper out from under the cushion. Why had Dad stuffed it there, and why didn't he want anyone to see it?

I glanced over the front page - nothing there out of the ordinary. On the second page there was a report about the Olympics. I sat down and started to read it. There was a lot of praise for someone they were calling 'the fastest man in the world'. I looked at his time for the 100 yards and it was only slightly faster than mine - on several occasions I had run the 100 yards almost as fast as he had, and the newspaper proclaimed that his was the fastest time ever recorded. The fastest man in the world? Not by much!

I put the newspaper back where I had found it under the cushion. I guess Dad thought that if I didn't see it I wouldn't get upset.

I suppose he was right. I never spoke to Mum or Dad about the report in the paper, and in fact, I didn't mention the Olympic Games to them ever again. After all, Dad was right, he wouldn't have had the money to buy cows if I had gone to the Olympic Games and we wouldn't now be thinking about calves coming along one day and owning a large herd.

* * *

It was the end of summer, the cows had settled down well and we were all looking forward to some new arrivals. Ben started to drop by regularly to see how we were getting on with the cows, and one day he brought his sister along with him.

"This is Mary" he said. "You don't mind her being here do you?"

"No" I said. Mary was quite a pretty girl, something which surprised me, as Ben had rather a big nose, his face was full of freckles and he wasn't at all good looking. We would spend hours staring at the cows, watching them chewing the grass and trying to keep out of the way of the bull.

Ben had a lovely horse, a piebald and very fast, so fast that when I went out with him across the fields on Bessie I couldn't keep up. In the late summer in our spare time Ben and I would put some pumpkins in a sack. When his dad wasn't looking we would go out into the fields and place the pumpkins about 10 yards apart on the ground and ride past them with sharpened sticks trying to stab the pumpkins while at full gallop. Our aim got pretty good, but Dad started to wonder where the pumpkins were disappearing to, and who was stealing them. We had to stop taking them, but we still managed to do our trick riding by placing some rags ten yards apart and seeing how many we could pick up at a gallop. We were becoming quite good at hanging down from the saddles by our legs and collecting the rags from the ground, until one day Ben fell off his horse.

I saw him double up in pain and galloped over to him.

"What's the matter, have you hurt yourself?"

"Yes, it's my leg, I heard a crack, I think I've broken it!" he panted. He was moaning in pain. I lifted his trouser leg up and saw that the upper part of his leg was facing in one direction and the bottom half in another. I was in no doubt that his leg was broken.

"Stay there" I said. "I'll go and get help."

"Well I can't go anywhere" Ben said. "Just be as quick as you can, I think I'm going to pass out."

I jumped on Bessie and galloped over the fields, through Barney's field and on down the lane to the Brown's farm. Mr Brown was coming across his field and was waving to me.

"Hello Charlie, I was just coming over to see your dad to find out how he's getting on" he said.

"He's OK Mr Brown, but its Ben, he's had an accident. His horse threw him and I think he has broken his leg."

I didn't dare tell Mr Brown what we had been up to for Ben to come off his horse.

"That's not like the pie. Where is Ben?"

"Over in the field beyond Mr Barney's."

"OK, I'll go and fetch the horse and cart, you go back to Ben."

I galloped back to where I had left Ben, and when I got there tears were running down his face. He was in real agony.

"Your Dad's coming Ben, he's just gone for the horse and cart. He'll be here in a few minutes" I told him.

"Don't you tell him what we were up to, otherwise he'll stop me riding" he said.

"Of course not, I just told him the pie had thrown you, that's all."

Ben was laid up for months while his leg was mending and I started to call on him regularly. I tried to give Mr Brown some help around his farm in my spare time. Although Ben's older brother John worked on the farm, I felt a little guilty and thought that it was my fault that Ben had fallen off his horse. Ben wasn't a daredevil, I was the one who had encouraged him to hang off the side of his horse and to sit on it backwards and try some new tricks.

The doctor re-set Ben's leg and plastered it up. He said

it was a clean break and time and rest would mend it, but he was not to put any weight on the leg whatsoever.

That put paid to our trick riding together for a while, although I couldn't resist taking Bessie out over the fields sometimes on my own to practise a little, as I had always thought that one day I might join a circus.

We always tried to finish early on Fridays, it sort of prepared us for the weekend, although we nearly always had to do some work on Saturday and Sunday mornings, but in spite of this I used to be full of anticipation of what the weekend might bring. One Friday Dad asked, "You going out, Charlie?"

"Yes, I'm going to see how Ben is getting on, it can't be much fun for him stuck up in that room of his day after day."

There was a knock on the door and Dad opened it. It was Harry.

"Hello Mr Carson, is Charlie in?"

"Yes, I'm in the kitchen Harry, what are you doing here?" I called.

"I've come to see you Charlie and to have a look at the cows, that's if you don't mind Mr Carson?"

Dad just looked at Harry. He was surprised to see him, as he had said repeatedly that he didn't want him anywhere near the farm and that I was to keep away from him. Dad looked at me and I went up to him and whispered to him that Harry had turned over a new leaf and was not getting into any trouble now.

"Well come on in then son, Charlie will take you out

to the field" Dad said to Harry. "I hope you're right about this" he muttered to me.

"I was just going out, but I'll take you out back first" I said.

"Where you going, Charlie?"

"I'm going over to see how Ben is doing, do you want to come? You know Ben Brown, don't you?"

"Yeah" he said. "He's a bit younger than me, but I do remember him from school. He's got a brother called John hasn't he?"

"Yeah that's right. Well he broke his leg and can't get out for a while."

I showed Harry the cows and told him they were expecting calves. He seemed a bit envious.

"You've got a proper farm now Charlie and the herd might become quite big in time" he said.

"Yeah, I hope so."

We headed off to see Ben and met Mr Brown coming out of his barn.

"Hello Mr Brown. How's Ben?"

"Pretty fed up with himself these days, not being able to get out and all. He's getting very depressed."

"This is my friend Harry Jenkins, he lives down by Westbury village."

"Hello son" he said. "Pleased to meet you."

"Hello Charlie" came a voice from behind me. It was Mary. I introduced her to Harry and I could see Harry was quite taken with her.

"I thought I might try and take Ben out, Mr Brown" I said.

"How you gonna manage to do that? You can't carry him and he can't ride a horse."

"Yes I know" I said. "Perhaps we could rig something up for him and wheel him about."

"Well you could try mending that old cart over there, I've got plenty of wood in the barn and I might even be able to find an old chassis if you boys want to give it a go."

"Sure we would, wouldn't we Harry? You'll give me a hand won't you?"

"Glad to be of help" said Harry.

John joined us and we set to repairing the cart for Ben to ride in. Mary was helping her dad bring the wood from the barn. He brought plenty of tools as well as nails, and we were all hammering and banging away until we had fashioned quite a good cart, even if I say so myself. It took us a while, but it was well worth it.

"Oil those wheels Charlie, they're squeaking quite a bit" Mr Brown said. With that done and Mr Brown putting the finishing touches, Mrs Brown came out to see what was going on. She soon went back inside the house and got some old bedding for the cart to make it more comfortable for Ben to sit on. Harry and I went into the house to carry Ben down from his room.

"What's all the commotion?" he said. "I could hear voices and banging. What's going on?"

"Come down and see for yourself." Harry got one side of Ben and I got the other and we carried him downstairs and out into the yard.

"Your carriage awaits you, my lord" I said, and

everyone started to laugh. Ben's face lit up as soon as he saw the cart-cum-carriage with two horses, which Mr Brown had harnessed to the front.

"You boys will have to drive the horses sitting on the edge of the cart" he said. "Later on I'll try and make some kind of seat. Meantime you had better try it out, but don't go too far."

We put Ben down on to the mattress that Mrs Brown had laid out in the back of the cart and Harry and I climbed up onto the front. Harry immediately jumped down from the cart and asked Mr Brown whether he could go to the barn for a sack of straw.

"Yes you can take some straw, as much as you want" he said.

He was back in no time at all with a sack which he had stuffed full. "Here Charlie" he said. "This will be more comfortable to sit on."

Mary jumped in with Ben and we took off up the lane, waving to Mr and Mrs. Brown and John as we went. We stopped off at my house and met Mum and Dad in the yard. They were both happy to see Ben out and about after so long. Mum disappeared for a while and came back holding a picnic basket.

"I've put some bread and cheese in this with some apples and lemonade" she said. "Now you drive carefully and have a nice time and make sure you're home before dark."

We drove off through the fields and stopped at a nice shady spot. Then we helped Ben out of the cart and sat him down, making him as comfortable as we could. Mary unpacked the picnic, laying out the cloth and pouring out the lemonade. Harry gave Mary a hand. It was obvious to Ben and me that Harry was quite smitten with Mary, but we tried not to notice when he touched her hand playfully as they were handing out the bread and cheese.

"I heard my dad talking to my brother last night about the war in the Balkans" said Ben. "It sounds really bad out there. My dad said first the Balkan States were fighting Turkey and now they have now turned on each other."

"Where are the Balkans?" asked Harry.

"Eastern Europe" said Ben.

"Well, maybe we'll be at war again one day ourselves" I said. "They say we're not getting on very well with Germany, it's something to do with trade and Kaiser Bill."

"Why does everybody keep talking about war? Can't you talk about something nice for a change?" said Mary.

"You're right Mary" I said. "Lets give it a rest."

I told them that when I had gone up to the city for Dad I had seen a lovely new motor car, called a Napier. It had six cylinders. When I spoke to a lad who was cleaning the car he said you could get them from 30 HP to 45 and even 65.

"What's HP?" asked Mary.

"Horsepower."

"How can it be a horse when it's a motor car?"

"Well, I believe that's how they measure the pulling power, comparing the car engine to a horse, I think. Maybe one day we'll all have motor cars."

"Stop dreaming" said Harry. "We'll be still riding around in our horse and carts when we're old, unless one of us gets rich, and I can't see that happening."

After we had had our lunch, Harry and I kicked a ball about and Mary joined in. Ben was laughing at Mary, because every time she kicked the ball she fell over. It seemed that when she kicked it she lost her balance, and a funnier sight you had never seen. She was forever picking herself up off the ground and dusting her long skirt down.

Harry kept rushing to her side giving her a helping hand. He demonstrated to her how it was possible to kick the ball and still remain standing. She got the hang of it, but we still fell about laughing.

At six o'clock we decided it was time to go home, as we didn't want to upset Mr Brown. If we were late back he might not let us bring Ben out again, and it would take us at least half an hour to get Ben and Mary back home.

Mr Brown was in his yard with Ben's brother John and Mrs Brown when we arrived back. Ben's brother lifted Ben out of the cart and took him inside the house. Ben waved goodbye to us from the doorway. Harry and I said our goodbyes to everyone and said we would be back another day to take Ben out again, and Mary thanked Harry and me for a lovely day.

Harry and I parted in the lane and said we would meet up the following weekend to go and see Ben and Mary.

Dad and I worked hard on the farm milking the cows and picking Brussels sprouts, digging up the last of the potatoes and clearing some of the land and replanting cabbages for the spring.

"I think we should have a greenhouse to grow cucumbers and tomatoes in next year" Dad said. "The tomatoes didn't do very well outside and if we had a greenhouse we wouldn't lose so many. With what we make from the milk now we can afford to buy the framing and glass. We'll have to build a brick enclosure first to put the framing on. How about giving me a hand to lay some bricks?"

"Well you'll have to show me how, I've never laid bricks before."

"Well now's your chance to learn. We'll start this weekend. We'll put it over there" Dad said, pointing to a sunny spot at the bottom of the vegetable field. "I'll order the stuff tomorrow so we can have it here for early Saturday morning."

"OK Dad" I said. "I'll just go and feed Bessie and then I'll come in for tea."

Well that's taken care of this weekend, I thought. I'll have to let Harry know that I can't take Ben out in the cart.

After I'd finished my tea I told Mum and Dad that I was going to see Harry to let him know I wouldn't be able to meet him this weekend. As I neared Harry's place, I could see him sitting on his front doorstep polishing what looked like a gun.

"Hello Harry, what's that you've got there?"

"It's only an airgun" he said. "Looks real, though doesn't it?"

"Yeah, it looks real to me. What you gonna do with that?"

"I told you, I'm going rabbiting. You want to come along?"

"Yeah, one day" I said. "By the way, I won't be able to meet you this weekend. Dad wants me to help him build a greenhouse, and I've got to learn how to lay bricks."

"Do you want me to give you a hand? I'm good at laying bricks, I learned it from my uncle. I think I'm quite good at it too."

"Well I'll ask Dad first, but I'm sure it will be all right. If we manage to get the bricks laid quickly, maybe by Sunday afternoon, we might still be able to take Ben out."

I mentioned to Dad that Harry had offered to give us a hand with the greenhouse. Dad was not too keen, but I assured him that Harry had definitely turned over a new leaf.

On Saturday morning Harry was banging on the door at 7.30 am. "Hello Mr Carson, hello Charlie, you ready to start work then, laying them bricks?"

"You're nice and early Harry" Dad said to him. "Come in and have a cup of tea, 'cause once we start mixing up the mortar there might not be time for a tea break for a few hours."

Harry sat down at the kitchen table and drank a cup of tea while Dad and I finished our breakfast.

"It's going to be a nice day today" said Harry. "There's not a cloud in the sky. You should be getting some calves pretty soon, I saw the bull chasing the cows around the field, he's quite frisky this morning."

"Good, I hope he is" replied Dad.

We worked hard all morning. Dad was mixing the mortar while keeping an eye on Harry and me laying the bricks. Harry was right when he said he could lay bricks, he was quick and neat, and every now and then he would come to the wall I was building and straighten the row I had laid and give me some good tips. Dad also laid some bricks when he wasn't mixing the mortar. We worked well together and we all laughed when Harry got carried away and built two extra rows his side of the wall, which Dad had to take off. Dad only wanted six rows and the glass framing had to go on top as soon as the mortar dried out.

"We can't do any more today" Dad said at last. "You can both take yourselves up to the house and get something to eat, and take the rest of the day off. I'll want a hand tomorrow though." He turned to me. "Charlie, I want a hand with the framing."

"OK Dad" I said, and Harry and I made our way up to the house. We washed our hands and changed our boots outside, so as not to upset Mum, as she had been cleaning all morning. Harry had brought some clean clothes to change into; I guess he knew what a mess we would be in after working with mortar.

I ran upstairs and washed my face and changed. After we'd eaten a nice stew that Mum had made, we headed off down the lane to see Ben. He was very glad to see us.

"I thought you were coming tomorrow" Ben said.

"We can't do any more to the greenhouse today" I said. "But my dad will need me tomorrow, so I thought we'd take you for a ride today if you want."

"Yes, that will be great."

We helped Ben get ready and Mary appeared when we were putting Ben in the cart. "Can I come as well?" she said.

"Sure" said Harry.

"I'll just leave a note for Dad then." Mary disappeared for a few minutes and came out carrying a blanket and a basket filled with bread, cakes and fruit juice.

"Mary's been baking this morning" said Ben. "She must have known you were coming round."

True to his word, Ben's Dad had fixed a seat to the front of the cart and after Harry and I harnessed two horses, which Ben's brother John had picked out from the field, we were off up the lane. Mary wanted to see some trick riding, so Harry and I unhitched the two horses. Harry was eager to impress Mary with his riding skills.

Harry and I galloped bareback in a race to the far side of the field and back again to see who was the fastest. It was more or less a tie. We then placed objects spaced out in two lines, such as the tea towel, the table cloth, jackets, caps and anything we could find, in the field, then galloped up to them and leaned down from the horses to pick them up and bring them back to where Ben and Mary sat.

Mary chose to shout and encourage Harry, and Ben shouted out, "Come on Charlie, Come on Charlie!" At one point Ben scrambled to his feet, forgetting about his leg, and leaned on his stick, waving his free hand in excitement.

I finished collecting all the items in my row first and

shortly after that Harry finished. We were both quite exhausted and fell to the ground laughing with excitement. Harry and I both loved horses and both hoped we could work with them for a living one day.

It was getting late, so we started to collect up all the things. We hitched up the horses to the cart, got Ben and Mary safely aboard and made our way back to Ben's house, singing at the tops of our voices. Ben's Dad was waiting for us and was glad to see that Ben was back to his old self again.

"You all sound as if you've had a good time" he said as he helped Ben down from the cart. "I don't think it will be long now before Ben's plaster comes off and he can go riding with you."

We said our farewells to Ben, Mary and Ben's Dad, and when Harry and I parted, he called back to me after going a few yards, "Do you want me to give you a hand with the rest of the greenhouse tomorrow?"

"Yeah" I said. "That will be great, if you have nothing else to do."

"See you tomorrow then."

"Yeah, but not too early."

"OK" said Harry, and he disappeared around the bend in the road.

Sunday morning Harry arrived at eight o'clock. Dad had already assembled some of the framework for the greenhouse. Dad and Harry were nailing up the main structure when I joined them. Harry and I helped Dad hoist up the side of the greenhouse with ropes. It all came together very quickly and by early afternoon we were standing back admiring our handiwork.

"Thank you both for giving me a hand, you've both worked hard" Dad said. "Come on up to the house."

We sat down and had something to eat. Mum had made us lots of pies, sandwiches and cakes.

"Here, take this" Dad said. He was holding out three shillings for Harry and three shillings for me. "Go and treat yourselves. Take yourselves off to the pictures tomorrow."

Harry and I had not been to see a film show in a long time, so on Monday afternoon we headed out over the fields running and jumping and yelling our heads off, we were so excited.

"What film are we going to see Charlie?" Harry said.

"I don't know. We'll have to see what's showing."

"Let's see one of those cowboy and Indian films."

"OK" I said. It was a pretty obvious choice for Harry and me. We managed to get into the picture palace after queuing for half an hour. We bought some sweets and made ourselves comfortable right in the middle row of the picture house.

Then a piano started to play and the words began to appear on the screen. Harry was not a fast reader, in fact his reading wasn't very good at all, so I read most of the lines out to him. It was very exciting when the Indians were chasing the cowboys and the arrows were flying. Harry could hardly keep still in his seat.

"That's some riding, hey Charlie! Did you see those

Indians jumping on to the horses and riding bareback, just like us?"

"Yeah, and did you see how they leaned down from their horses to pick up the guns and rifles from the ground that the dead cowboys had dropped, just like we do" I said.

"I'd like to be a cowboy Charlie, rounding up all those cattle and driving them for miles across the prairie, sleeping out at night under the stars."

"Yeah, that's OK if its not raining" I said.

For weeks after we had seen the film all Harry and I wanted to do was to ride and practise our skills with the horses. Harry had managed to buy a horse from Ben's Dad, on a sort of have now, pay later basis. Ben's dad was really grateful to both of us for taking Ben out in the cart and keeping his spirits up when his leg was in plaster. As soon as Ben was fit and able to ride he joined Harry and me out in the fields riding and jumping over hedges.

The winter set in early and the dark nights seemed very long. I hated getting up in the mornings to work on the land, which was more often than not frozen and as hard as a rock. We had stopped the digging months before and were only able to collect the winter vegetables and take them to market during this time and clear up the fields. My fingers froze and ached with the cold.

I tried to exercise Bessie when she was well enough. She had caught a chill and for a long time we thought she might die. The vet didn't hold out much hope, and said that all we could do for her was to try to keep her warm and comfortable during the bad weather. Every night I checked that the small oil heater was turned up high. I had nailed extra planks of wood all round the barn to try to keep out as many draughts as I could; although it was a new barn that Dad had built, I wasn't taking any chances.

It was spring before Bessie was really well again and I was able to stop worrying about her. Dad had employed two young lads to help on the land with the digging and planting and I managed the livestock, but I was not happy, and I was getting bored with the farm.

Harry and I met up regularly and now that the weather had improved we decided to ride again, but I had to borrow a horse from Ben's dad because Bessie was still not at her best.

One lovely spring morning at breakfast, Dad said "Look at this." Mum and I looked up and he was holding up the newspaper.

"Why don't you go along with your mates to see this exhibition?" he said to me. He handed me the newspaper and I saw that it was advertising a 'Wild West Exhibition' to be held at the White City Stadium in London. Colonel W. F. Cody, better known as Buffalo Bill, was coming to town with a large troupe of cowboys and Indians.

Everyone had heard of Buffalo Bill. I jumped up without finishing my breakfast, ran upstairs, splashed some water on my face and rushed over to show Harry the newspaper. He was jumping up and down when I told him Buffalo Bill was coming to London.

We both raced over to see Ben and showed him the newspaper. Mary was there, and John. We all began to run round the kitchen table making Indian noises and doing an Indian war dance. Ben picked up a chopper, making out it was a tomahawk, and chased us round the table.

Hearing all the commotion, Ben's mum and dad came in, and at first they were horrified to see Ben running around with a chopper in his hand. But we laughed out loud and assured them that their son had not gone crazy. We showed them the newspaper.

"Well that's fantastic" said Ben's dad. "Just what you boys need. But you best get tickets early. I can imagine there will be a great stampede."

We all decided that we must get the tickets right away, as we didn't intend to miss this exhibition. Ben's Dad said he would pay for all of us to go, as we had looked after Ben when he broke his leg and he was very grateful to us all.

"I want to come too" Mary said.

Ben's Dad disappeared and came back a few minutes later holding out two gold sovereigns, which he gave to John to go and buy the tickets. "You had better take Charlie with you just in case you meet up with robbers. Bring me back the change, son" he said.

John got his horse out of the stable and Ben brought his out for me to ride. Then we took off across the fields, whooping and cheering and waving as we went. We couldn't wait for the big day to arrive. We were all really excited, as none of us had ever been to a live show, let alone one as spectacular as this.

When the big day arrived we were in our seats before anyone else. The stadium started to fill up and the crowds were so huge that there was not a seat left empty in the whole of the stadium.

When Buffalo Bill finally entered the arena, the cheers were deafening. Almost everyone wanted to be a cowboy, and many dreamed of being an Indian scout. He was such a great idol that some of the lads had tears in their eyes.

He was followed into the arena by at least two dozen cowboys and as many Indians. There were stagecoaches and Pony Express riders, and women shootists. There were also Cossacks from Russia and Syrian and Arabian horsemen. Before long the arena was full to the brim with beautiful horses and riders, the likes of which we had never seen. The sight was almost overwhelming.

The troupe left the arena, and there was silence for a few seconds. Then the Deadwood Mail Coach came thundering in, followed a few seconds later by screaming and howling Indians firing arrows into it and chasing it around the arena. Then in came Buffalo Bill and the cowboys, whooping and shooting the Indians. The audience were all cheering and shouting and waving their arms and clapping.

The Cossacks came in next. They were great horsemen, showing off their skills and doing all sorts of riding feats.

"Look" said Harry. "That's what we've been doing, hanging down from the saddles and jumping on and off our horses."

Then there were the Pony Express riders, showing how they rode across the prairie passing mail from one rider to the other without stopping or dropping anything, so as to get the mail delivered as quickly as possible. I was later told that the best riders could cover as much as fifty or sixty miles in one day.

Then Annie Oakley rode into the arena on her horse firing her pistols. She was a crack shot and her horse skills and marksmanship received huge applause.

Finally the cowboys came back into the arena showing off their skills and racing each other to great applause. Then they invited members of the audience to come down into the arena and take part.

"Go on Charlie, go down and have a go. You show 'em what you can do!" said Harry.

"No" I said. "I want to watch the show."

Harry had spotted a friend in the audience, a boy called Tom Watson, who ran down the aisle. Harry ran down after him with other lads to join in the fun. Some were given the chance to race with the cowboys and others rode bareback on horses of the Indians. Nearly all fell off, to huge laughter from the crowds. Some managed to stay on, but by the time the horses were pulled up the volunteers were barely hanging on round the horses' necks.

Finally the whole troupe came back into the arena and we all cheered until we were hoarse. We had had so much fun that we didn't want the show to end.

On the way home Harry said he wanted to train to ride like the Cossacks and he asked me what I would like to do.

"I want to be a Pony Express rider and ride out over the prairie, delivering mail, that's what I would like to do most" I said. "I don't want to be a cowboy any more, or join a circus now. I want an important job and I want to travel from place to place and see different parts of the country, getting the mail through. It's great receiving letters and packages."

John and Ben were both wanting to be fine shots and were impressed by the shooting competitions. Mary said she had had such a great time that she was just happy to watch all the performances and was really glad she came along.

For days afterwards we spoke about nothing else but Buffalo Bill's Exhibition. Mum and Dad were enthralled listening to me relating the whole show to them. Everyone wanted to hear about it wherever we went, as few people were lucky enough to get tickets. We all thanked Ben's dad for the treat, and he was happy that we had enjoyed ourselves.

As the months passed by I became listless and told Harry and Ben I had decided to join the army.

"You can't!" Ben said. "You're not old enough."

"Well, if you two don't say anything and no one else knows, who's going to tell?" I said.

"Your mum and dad for a start" said Harry. "And what about the farm? Your Dad needs you there."

"No he doesn't" I said. "The two new helpers are all he needs."

"I bet he stops you" said Ben.

"I'll be gone before he can do anything about it" I said.

"But you're only fifteen" said Ben.

"No, I'm nearly sixteen. I'll be sixteen in November."

"Well, that's a long way off yet."

"They say a war might start soon and I want to be ready and fully trained if there is one. I don't want to be hanging around" I said.

"When do you plan to go?" asked Harry.

"By the end of May."

"Well that's only about two weeks from now" said Ben.

"Yeah, so you only have two weeks to keep quiet about it. That's not too much to ask, is it?"

"Of course, Ben and I won't say a word to anyone, will we Ben?" said Harry.

"No no, not a word" said Ben.

"What regiment do you think you will join, Charlie?" asked Harry.

"Oh, I don't know, I suppose I'll have to go wherever they put me, but my choice would be the cavalry. Tell you what, I'll say goodbye to you both today so that you two are completely above suspicion, and I'll see you one day when I come home, whenever that will be."

"OK Charlie" said Ben. "I'll miss you."

"So will I, Charlie" said Harry. "I'll miss riding with you, things won't be the same without you."

"Say goodbye to Mary for me, but don't let her know where I've gone, at least not for a few months" I said to Ben.

It was a sad parting. We had all grown very close and we were the best of pals.

Chapter Four

For the next two weeks I planned to stay close to home except for joining up, which took a bit longer than I thought, but by the second week of June 1913, I was one of His Majesty's soldiers serving in the British Armed Forces. As I had said I wanted to be working with horses I managed to get the sort of job I had hoped for, working close to the cavalry. It wasn't much of a job though. I thought I would be riding the thoroughbreds, but instead I was just mucking out the stables and feeding the horses, when I wasn't polishing Lieutenant Cranleigh's boots.

It was on one such afternoon when I was polishing the boots that Captain Wilcox stopped in front of me. I jumped up and saluted him, letting the boots fall to the ground.

"You're Carson, aren't you?" he said.

"Yes sir" I replied.

"How are the horses doing? I hear the dapple grey has caught a chill."

"Yes sir, but I've given her a good rub down and she should be as right as rain tomorrow."

"Well done, Carson. Can you ride?"

"Oh yes sir!" I replied eagerly.

"I don't mean can you manage to stay in the saddle for a little while. When I say can you ride, I mean for hours at a time without feeling sore or falling out of the saddle."

"Yes sir, I can. I did a lot of riding on the farm at home sir. Had my own horse." I wondered where he wanted me to go, perhaps on an errand somewhere that would take a few hours.

"I'd like to see you ride, Carson. There's a race on Saturday with some of the top horsemen in the Cavalry. Would you like to enter the race?"

"Yes sir. I am sure I'm as good as any man here, and I'm sure I can give any of the Cavalry a run for their money, providing I have a half decent horse, sir."

The Captain began to laugh out loud.

"Well you are a modest fellow, aren't you!" he said sarcastically. "The race is at ten on Saturday morning. Try to find yourself a half-decent horse and lets see what you can do, Private Carson."

"Yes sir, thank you sir."

"Pick out a horse of your choice from that bunch over there and make sure you're at the starting line promptly on Saturday. I'll know then if you're just boasting, won't I? Don't let me down, Carson!"

"I won't sir."

After the Captain left I sat down on a bale of hay and looked at the Lieutenant's boots, which were still lying on the ground. I picked them up and finished polishing them. I thought to myself, I don't have any riding boots like these. Maybe I was too boastful after all, my riding skills were one thing, but having the right gear and the right horse was another.

I went out in the field after I had finished my chores and gave the horses a look over. I couldn't see a single horse which looked suitable to ride in the race. I was wondering what I was going to do when Ginger appeared. Ginger Metcalf was the first real friend I had made since joining up.

"What you doing over here? Thinking of doing a bit of horse trading when you leave the army?"

"Oh, hello Ginger. I've been given the chance to ride in the race on Saturday by Captain Wilcox, if I can find myself a horse, that is."

"Well it was only the other day that I let slip to Lieutenant Cranleigh how well you can ride and what a great horseman you are. I guess he told the Captain."

"I did wonder why he gave me the opportunity to race."

"I think they're looking for a few good horsemen to join the despatch riders. I suppose if you do well they may consider you."

"Despatch riders?"

"Yes, that's what I said. What do you think? Can you see yourself as a despatch rider?"

"Yes, that would be great. That would really be great! A proper job, instead of mucking out the horses and cleaning boots. I was wondering why the Captain asked me if I could stay in the saddle for a long time. That explains it."

"Well I still need a horse. Any ideas where I am going to get one?"

"Sure" said Ginger. "Let's go look over the Cavalry officers' horses and see what we can find."

"You must be mad. If I take one of those I'll really be in trouble."

"Well, let's go and see first" said Ginger.

The Cavalry horses were kept in a different field and were solely for the officers' use. Not like the lot we had just been looking over, which were kept mainly for pulling carts. Ginger and I went round to the stables and found Angus, a friend of Ginger's, who was a giant of a man from Scotland. I don't know whether Ginger was joking when he said Angus' father had named him after his prize bull. He was busy shoeing a horse and was so engrossed in what he was doing that we just stood and watched him for a few seconds before he turned round, rather startled.

"What are you doing here?" he said.

Ginger introduced me to him and told him I could race on Saturday if I could find a horse good enough to ride. "You got a horse Charlie can borrow?" he asked. "One that's not already racing and won't be missed?"

"None at all, sorry son" said Angus. "I cannae help ye there."

I went to sleep that night thinking, if only I had kept my big mouth shut, I would be far better off. It was Tuesday the next day and I had just four days to find a horse of the stature and fitness to enter the race. I could use my ordinary army boots, but I did need to find a saddle from somewhere just in case a horse was found that I could ride.

In the morning I mentioned to a couple of the lads what had transpired between Captain Wilcox and myself and they couldn't believe he had given me a chance to ride in the race on Saturday with all the top brass. Freddie Peters, one of Angus' friends, said, "Oh, it's because they are short of numbers and it makes them all look good by beating the inexperienced riders."

He had never seen me ride. In fact only Ginger knew how well I could ride.

"Pinch one of the Cavalry horses" Freddie said.

"Oh, I can't do that. I'll get thrown in the stockade. Something may turn up in the next few days" I replied. I really couldn't see how, but I was keeping my fingers crossed.

It was Thursday afternoon when Ginger put his head round the stable door and threw a pair of boots at my feet.

"Eights, is that right? Size eights?"

I looked at him. rather startled.

"You do take eights, don't you?"

I couldn't believe my eyes. Ginger had brought me a pair of boots.

"They're not new. They were in for repairs. No one's gonna miss them for a while. You wear them on Saturday, then you can give them back to me, OK?"

"Thanks Ginger" was all I could manage to say.

"I'm working on the saddle, and of course the horse. There's still a couple of days yet. Who knows what will turn up." With that he disappeared round the stable door.

I didn't see Ginger again until Friday afternoon. He

came into the stable leading a horse, fully saddled. She was a brown mare with very distinctive white markings down her nose and a white mane, and two white forelegs.

"Here, you had better take her for a ride" he said. "You haven't got much time, the race being tomorrow and all."

"Who does she belong to?" I asked.

"Nobody yet. All I can say is she's one of the new recruits, one of the new consignment of a dozen horses that have just arrived, and she's the best of the bunch."

"Won't they ask me where I got her?"

"Don't worry about that. There's no paperwork yet on the new horses, at least none that can be found, and there won't be until well after the race. Same goes for the saddle. Now get going. Try her out, but don't wear her out."

I rode off on the mare, straight out of the cantonment and into the open countryside. She was very frisky and just wanted to gallop. I gave her her head and she took off like lightning. I rode for several hours, getting to know her and letting her get to know me. It was past seven o'clock when I returned to the stable. I fed and watered the horse, which I now had named Mabel. I put her in one of the stalls at the back of the stable, just in case anyone passing might spot her.

That night I could hardly sleep for excitement. I had to win the race. I was going to win the race. That's all I could think of. I *must* win the race!

I woke early and got some of my chores done before breakfast. I was down in the stables saddling Mabel when Ginger arrived at nine o'clock.

"Not long to go now, Charlie. How's the mare?"

"Oh she's fine, just look at her, she's in fine spirits. I think she'll run a good race today."

"Good" said Ginger. "Best get out of here early just in case - sort of make yourself scarce for a while. Some of the officers may get a bit jealous if they see you with the mare before the race and try to prevent you from riding her. Just make sure you're at the starting line at ten o'clock – yeah?"

"OK Ginger. I'm out of here. See you after the race."

I took a detour round the back of the stables and slipped out of the cantonment and out of sight as quickly as I could. I kept Mabel at a slow canter for a while, and then let her go at full gallop for a short distance. She seemed to be full of the joys of spring and really wanted to take off.

I walked with her for some time, trying to keep her as relaxed as possible, talking to her all the while. I hadn't realized that the time had passed so quickly, and glancing at my watch, I knew I had better make it back, otherwise the race would be over before I got there.

The riders were all at the starting line and I fell in behind them all, keeping back a short distance. I saw some of the officers looking over their shoulder, eyeing Mabel up and down, and I heard mutterings.

"She looks a fine mare" one officer said.

"Not seen her before" said another.

No one had set eyes on Mabel before of course, and there were surprised looks on a lot of faces.

The tape was raised and we were off. Some of the

officers went off at full gallop, but I kept Mabel at the back of the riders and held her at a steady pace, as we had two and a half miles to race and there would be plenty of time to push her forward as the race progressed.

After several furlongs Mabel was wanting to speed up, and I felt her tugging on the reins. I released the reins a bit more and we were soon passing one rider after another until there were only four horses out in front of us. I could tell Mabel was not happy trailing them and she let me know, tugging hard on the reins.

I gave her her head and she took off like the wind to catch them up. We passed one, two and then three. Now there was only one more to catch and we soon came up level with the rider. It was Lieutenant Brown. I had heard about him. Apparently he had a vicious temper, and I had been advised early on, when I had first arrived at the camp, to keep well clear of him. He was mean and had a reputation for brutality.

We raced neck and neck for two furlongs with Lieutenant Brown whipping his horse furiously, but he could not keep pace with us, and Mabel sped past. We passed the winning post several yards clear.

There was cheering and shouting all around us and Mabel reared up. Maybe she was taking a bow in her own way. She seemed proud and triumphant, as if she ran races regularly. She kicked up her back legs as if to say "How about that then?"

"Well done Charlie!" I heard a voice say, and turning around I saw Ginger smiling from ear to ear. "Well done mate" he said. It was almost like being back in the boxing ring when everyone was cheering me, but this time I wasn't in pain and bruised all over with my eyes swelling up and my nose pouring with blood. I was fit and well, and so was Mabel. It was a great feeling.

Much to my surprise, Lieutenant Brown came up and patted me on the back.

"That's the first time I've lost this race in four years" he said. "Well done, private."

"Thank you sir" I said, hardly believing what I had just heard. Maybe the rumours were unfounded; maybe he wasn't such a bad bloke after all.

Ginger grabbed the reins and told me to dismount and go and collect the prize money. I hadn't thought about any prize, I was just happy to have taken part in the race. The race organiser thrust four gleaming white five-pound notes into my hand. "Well done Carson" he said.

I had never had twenty pounds before. In fact I had never *seen* twenty pounds before, and I could hardly believe my eyes. So much money! It was a fortune. I felt like a millionaire. All that money for doing something I loved.

I was so excited and happy that as soon as I got back to the barracks I sat down and wrote a letter to Mum and Dad. I had only written to them once since I had left home, and that was just a brief note to say I was well and for them not to worry about me.

After I had brought Mum and Dad up to date with all my news I stuffed the twenty pounds in the envelope and added a PS: "I hope the enclosed money will help with the farm and please buy yourselves something nice as well. All my love, Charlie".

I had just finished my letter when Ginger came through the door.

"How you feeling Charlie. On cloud nine I suppose?"

"Yeah, I can't believe I beat all those officers."

"Well just because they are high ranking doesn't mean they're good at everything. Anyway I need to take the boots back Charlie, before they're missed, and Mabel."

"OK Ginger. Thanks again for all your help." I took off the boots and handed them to him.

"Oh think nothing of it Charlie. What are mates for?"

★ ★ ★

The next morning I was woken by someone tugging at my shoulder.

"Get up Carson! Captain Wilcox wants to see you sharp at 08.30." It was Lieutenant Cranleigh's orderly.

"What does he want me for?" I asked.

"I don't know. He doesn't exactly confide in me. I'm just carrying out orders."

I quickly washed and shaved and rushed to the canteen for some breakfast as there was still a little while to go yet.

The orderly was sitting outside the Captain's office when I arrived, and he jumped up and knocked on the Captain's door.

"Come in" said the Captain. When I saw Lieutenant

Cranleigh in the room with the Captain, I thought I was in big trouble about Mabel, the saddle and the boots.

"You rode a splendid race yesterday Carson - congratulations again" said the Lieutenant.

"Thank you sir" I said.

"You're probably wondering why I have called you here. I'll get straight to the point. We're looking for recruits who can ride well to become despatch riders, and it seems you fit the bill. If you remember, I asked you a few days ago whether you could stay in the saddle for long periods at a time, and that's what you would have to do if you are picked to be one of our despatch riders. We only want the best riders to apply, and in my opinion you are one of our finest riders."

"Thank you sir" I said.

"You can think it over for a few days and let Lieutenant Cranleigh know your decision. Of course the recruits that sign up early will get first pick from the bunch of horses which have just arrived, so I shouldn't leave it too long to make up your mind. You have great potential, and I'm sure after a few months training you will be a great asset to the regiment."

"I would definitely like to be a despatch rider, sir. I don't have to think about it."

My mind was racing ahead. If I decided on the spot, I could pick Mabel to be my mount, and nothing would please me more.

"Well if you're sure. There are a few formalities to take care of - forms to fill out etc., then you can go off to select your horses."

"Horses, sir?"

"Yes, you will need to select two. Each despatch rider needs two horses, just in case one goes lame. You'll be trained to ride with two horses at all times. Choose carefully, as these horses will be your companions and maybe your life savers, should we go to war, the likelihood of which seems evermore increasing as the days go by."

After filling out the necessary forms I made my way over to the pasture where the new horses were grazing. Ginger was there and I told him what had happened.

"That's great" he said. "If only I could ride half as good as you, that's what I would want to do. Let's find Mabel if you want her, and we'll pick another good mare. They need to be compatible. It's no good if the horses don't get on."

Ginger and I found Mabel and another young mare she seemed to like, and one we certainly took a fancy to. She was very dark grey with a white patch on her nose.

"Well I won't have to pinch a saddle for you this time" said Ginger. "You'll be allocated boots, saddles, the lot. I'll come with you to the stores when you get your requisition form. Meantime get your horses in the stable and give them a good rub down. I'll see you later."

I put Mabel and Sue – yes, I thought, Sue is a nice name, that's what I'll call her - into the stables and began working on them. All my other chores had ceased from today and tomorrow I would start my first day of training.

After lunch an orderly came by with my requisition form and I found Ginger already in the supplies store. He helped me carry out the saddles and all the gear I was allotted.

"You'd better get your name put on some of this gear" he said. "There are a lot of light-fingered people around here."

Lieutenant Cranleigh's orderly poked his head round the stable at 5 pm. "Captain Wilcox wants you and all the other despatch riders assembled at 0700 hours in the field just off the Parade Ground with horses fully saddled" he said. "From there you will be taken north for your training with both your mounts." With that he turned and was gone.

I wasn't sure whether I had heard right. Did he say both mounts? To be ready by seven I would have to be up very early to get myself ready and both the horses, maybe as early as five. I started to smile. I would be getting up at the same time as our cockerel at home.

Things were moving very fast. I could hardly believe I was being called a despatch rider already. I was overjoyed, and my heart was racing, all my dreams of being a rider were coming true.

I couldn't sleep that night. I had gone to bed early, but tossed and turned all night. At 4.30 am I jumped out of bed and began to wash and shave. Although I only had a few sparse hairs on my chin, it made me feel more mature to shave like the older blokes.

It was 6.30 when I led Mabel and Sue out onto the field which was to be the meeting point for all the riders. There was no one there, but I was pleased, as I could try to settle the horses with no one around. I didn't realise how difficult it was to keep two horses in check. One was pulling this way and the other that way. I had to keep reining Sue in, as although she got on well with Mabel, she didn't necessarily want to be that close to her all the time. It took me a while to adjust the reins and to get Sue into a position where she was more comfortable.

Before long one rider after the other was arriving. Most of them were having trouble with their mounts. There were twelve riders and 24 horses. I didn't know most of the riders and only had a nodding acquaintance with perhaps three of them.

Mabel and Sue became very unsettled with the bucking horses, so I took them off a short distance for a canter and returned to see Captain Wilcox and Lieutenant Cranleigh on the field. Captain Wilcox ordered everyone to dismount. The horses did become a little calmer, but there were still many riders having difficulty with their mounts.

There was a roll call: "Adams?" "Sir!" "Brown?" "Sir!" "Carson?" "Sir!" "Faraday?" "Sir!" "Ferguson?" "Sir!" "Heywood?" "Sir!" The names became a bit of a blur after a while, as I was still having trouble keeping Mabel and Sue calm.

"We'll be riding or walking as the case may be for six miles, and I expect you all to keep up" said Captain Wilcox. The order was given to 'Mount Up'. I was up on Mabel in an instant and followed the Captain and the Lieutenant out of the field and onto the road. I glanced back after a few moments to see that the majority of the riders were mounted and following behind, but there were one or two still having difficulty with their horses and just leading them by their reins.

By the time we reached the training centre most of the riders were managing their horses quite well and each pair of horses were getting used to trotting alongside each other.

Over the next ten weeks we were trained how to ride our mounts properly, how to tether our horses together and how to jump onto the horses within seconds, how to dismount before the horses came to a standstill and how to rein them in in tight formation very close together until both horses were acting as one, as we would need complete control in case we found ourselves under heavy artillery fire. It was paramount that we got through with the despatches; if we lost one horse we would have to jump up on to the other.

The training was very intensive and if you didn't have good riding skills and lots of experience with horses, you were clearly not going to make the grade. At the end of it all only five of us of twelve recruits did well enough to become despatch riders.

Chapter Five

The months went by and I was really very happy being around horses all the time, training with them, feeding them and grooming them. I began taking despatches to different cantonments. I was happiest when I was out in the open fields riding my mounts, and in anyone's eyes I was a fully-grown man doing his duties in the army.

The summer of 1914 was extremely hot, hotter than I could ever remember. On August 4th it was declared that we were at war with Germany and its allies, Austria and Hungary. We had heard that Austria had already invaded Serbia, after the assassination of Archduke Franz Ferdinand in Sarajevo in June. Kaiser Bill had amassed his armies and the German soldiers had crossed into Belgium in no time at all, and by September they had pushed into France in the north at Thiepval, taking the château. They were at Ovillers and Mametz, and in the south they were close to Verdun. The French army were taking heavy casualties, being mown down by artillery and machine-gun fire.

There was a rumour that we would soon be transported out. We were not yet sure of our destination, but Verdun was mentioned in several conversations that were overheard by the men. The French were seeking our assistance there and it was rumoured that a large contingent of the British Army would be heading down that way.

We were asked to be ready to be shipped out at short notice, but nothing happened for quite a while.

One day I got a letter from Mum and Dad thanking me for the money. They were facing hard times, as most of the farmhands had joined the army following Lord Kitchener's appeal for people to join up. They had heard from Bert, who was in India, but he had been separated from Fred for a long while and wasn't sure where he was. Everyone else was just fine. Mary and Ben had been over to see them several times. Ben hadn't passed the medical for the army and was very upset about it, but he was glad to know that I had been able to get a job working with horses. It was nice receiving a letter from home and to know that every one was OK.

Fancy that, Bert in India. Well he was better off out of it. I only hoped Fred was well clear of all this trouble in Europe as well.

It was not until late September that our orders came to say that our regiment was being shipped out to France. Our destination wasn't known until we were crossing the Channel, when we heard that we were actually headed for the Somme and to Verdun.

I had to take charge of the horses and to see that they were safely tethered on board ship and that their food was safely stored. I was the only despatch rider with this regiment and I seemed to get slightly better treatment than the other privates.

I began to hear terrible stories about the casualties in France. The French troops were sustaining heavy losses, in fact they were talking not of tens of soldiers or hundreds, but thousands of soldiers were being killed every day.

When we landed on French soil it was very early in the morning and it was a bright sunny day. I was immediately sent off with a despatch. I had been given maps of the Somme which I had been studying on the ship, trying to acquaint myself with the terrain, and Ginger had given me a compass – "just in case you get lost", he had said. I had a canteen of water and food ration for a day.

With the strap of my despatch bag swung over my head and the bag safely on my back, I mounted Mabel. I could immediately tell that she and Sue were glad to be off the ship and happy to feel solid ground beneath their hooves once more. They sniffed the air and snorted loudly as if to say, "This place smells different".

I marvelled at the beauty of the French countryside. The field I was crossing was covered with wild flowers – there were whites, blues and yellows and the vibrant reds of millions of poppies scattered across the landscape. Mary would have been overjoyed at the sight of so many pretty flowers.

Mary! I kept seeing her pretty, smiling face. Why did I keep thinking about her? Maybe the letter from Mum and

Dad had made me remember her. How I missed everyone back home!

There was just a light breeze, but I could sense something different in the air. There was an eerie silence as I rode along, and after a while I realized that I couldn't see any birds or hear them singing. I let the horses go at a slow canter while I was trying to get my bearings. I had to head south. I checked my map, my compass and my watch, and adjusted the reins of both horses.

I rode until nightfall, when the silence was broken by what sounded like thunder far in the distance. Of course I knew it was not thunder, as there was a clear starry night sky. It was the distant sound of artillery fire. It was very far off, and the noise was probably being carried on the wind,

I had ridden all day with just one short break to give the horses a rest; I had almost reached our headquarters, which was north of Amiens, which I calculated to be about a quarter of the way to Verdun. I found myself a nice spot to spend the night and let the horses graze nearby. I was confident that they would not wander off, and even if they did they would not go far and would come running as soon as I whistled for them. I had learned that it was best not to tether them. First they could munch away at the grass wherever they pleased, and secondly, in an emergency I could take off on the back of one without worrying about untying them, as the other would automatically follow.

I awoke the next morning being nuzzled by Sue; it was

her way of telling me to get up. It was as if she could tell the time and wanted to be off. It was just getting light, and the air was cool and quiet.

On reaching the headquarters north of Amiens, I was sent off almost immediately to Verdun, which was at least a two-and-a-half-day ride away. On my second night out I slept in some bushes in scrubland on the edge of a forest.

It was about three in the morning when I was awoken by Mabel snorting and stamping. When I looked around to see what was disturbing her I saw something moving a few feet away to my left. At first I could not make out what it was, but then I saw the two big razor-sharp tusks in the moonlight, and realised it was a wild boar. I jumped up immediately and reached for my knife, but as I did so the animal took off into the woods.

I decided to leave the area as quickly as possible. As I was mounting up I heard a shot from the woods and loud voices, not in English. I guessed that the boar had run into the Hun. The animal had done me a big favour by alerting me to more serious dangers nearby.

I set off in a south-easterly direction. I still had a long ride in front of me before reaching our headquarters near Verdun. When I got there I handed over the despatches and was shown where I could get something to eat and where to put the horses for the night. I was told I would have to start off very early the next morning, before sun up. I would be going closer to the enemy lines, so close in fact that on the map it looked as if the English, French and Germans were all but sharing the same trenches.

I bedded down early after making sure the horses were fed and watered, hoping that the distant artillery fire would not disturb them too much. We were much closer to the enemy now and only a few miles behind our own lines. I soon fell asleep, and before I knew it someone was calling out my name.

"Carson, wake up! Carson, it's time you were off."

I just had time to wet my face and put on a clean pair of socks. Mum had told me it was important always to keep my feet dry.

It was 4.30 am. The sky was overcast and it was starting to rain. I put some rations in my saddlebag and before mounting up I threw on my waterproof cape, as it was essential to keep as dry as possible; riding hour after hour in the rain you could really get soaked, and I didn't want to get stiff joints.

I rode Sue to give Mabel a rest - I planned to alternate the mounts throughout my time out there. I would be depending on my own riding skills to stay alive, but first and foremost, I would be depending on the horses.

When I reached our forward lines I found it difficult to control the horses, as there was heavy machine gun fire coming from half a mile or so up ahead. I gave my despatch to the Captain and rode out of there as fast as I could with another despatch for the headquarters at Verdun. It seemed from the conversations I was overhearing that more British troops were needed. I wondered just how many of our boys had been killed already and how many more they were willing to sacrifice.

It was early evening before I was given another despatch. I had grabbed an hour's sleep while waiting to be sent out again. Unless there was a quick turn around, I always tried to rest up as much as possible, as I never quite knew when I would get some sleep again, or eat for that matter. However late at night or early in the morning it was, I would be sent off with another despatch and sometimes I would have to ride great distances.

I was now ordered to take a despatch to our position south-west of Mametz, as it appeared that despatches weren't getting through up there. It would be a long hard ride to a different area of engagement. I thought I would make a big detour and head in a westerly direction, then turn north when I was far away from these battlegrounds, all the while keeping well away from the enemy lines near Verdun. I would head up to the Somme river and on to our headquarters, which was several miles south-west of Mametz. I wondered why I wasn't being sent off this morning, but I guessed the Colonel had his reasons. Maybe he thought I would be safer under the cover of darkness.

I was tightening Mabel's saddle strap and getting ready to leave when all hell broke loose. An Adjutant ran towards me. "Get out of here Carson, we are pulling back!" he said. "Get going. The Hun have broken through our lines."

I was quickly up on Mabel and heading out of there with artillery fire bursting all around me. Everything was being blasted, and it was difficult to keep the horses reined in. The terrain was changing all the time. One minute I could just about see a clump of trees to my left, the next they had been obliterated.

I headed west, hoping to keep out of reach of the artillery fire. After an hour I stopped to refer to my map. I seemed to have lost my bearings a bit. In my estimation I was now well away from enemy lines, so even after their advance they should still be well south of me and I should be able to continue in a westerly direction.

Night had now fallen and the artillery fire had at last stopped. I felt a bit easier now, and the horses had settled down. I surveyed the area and could just see a small clump of trees at the back of some open ground. I rode on a short way and found that beyond the trees was a long ditch and then open ground again. As it had now become very dark and there was no moonlight, only very heavy clouds, and I wasn't sure of my direction, I decided to make a bed for the night in the ditch and be off at first light. I felt around and found some branches, which I threw into the ditch just in case it was wet. I then laid down my waterproof and placed my despatch bag down for a pillow. The horses were grazing nearby, so I pulled a few more branches over me to keep out any chill or rain and went to sleep.

I awoke with the rain spitting on my face. Without moving I looked up through a gap in the branches and saw broken clouds. Maybe it was just an isolated shower.

I was about to get up when I heard voices and a trickle of water. I strained my ears trying to hear what was being said, but they were not speaking in English. There was the sound of more water, then a familiar unpleasant smell - urine. It now dawned on me that I was in the German lines and that they were using the ditch as a latrine.

The smell became more and more intense as the soldiers relieved themselves one after another. I knew that if I moved I would be shot or bayoneted. I just had to lie there in all that stench.

One soldier was urinating near my boots. As I watched him through a small gap in the branches I could see a very large spider leaving the ditch and crawling up the soldier's right trouser leg. He saw the spider and gave out a shriek, knocking it to the ground. He then stamped on it several times and kicked it back into the ditch. It fell on some leaves above my chest, writhing and oozing its innards.

The soldier called out to his comrades and I guessed that he was warning them of spiders and snakes. One soldier about two feet away from my head started to thrust his bayonet into the ditch, and it struck a branch near the top of my head. The blade of his bayonet missed my head but pierced the edge of my despatch bag. Satisfied that he would have killed any snakes or spiders in that patch, he relieved himself in a big way. The stench was overpowering.

After a while the voices died down and I could only just hear them in the distance. I could smell coffee in the air and almost immediately the British artillery shells started raining down. I pulled myself up and looked around. The Germans were running around like headless chickens darting this way and that trying to take cover as the shells rained down. Then they disappeared down holes in the ground like moles.

I had got behind the enemy lines all right, but I hadn't planned to be this close to their trenches, which were just in front of the line of trees. I had thought they were several miles south of me, not a few yards.

I gathered my stuff together and looked around for the horses. I could just see them between the trees; they had been tethered close together. The Germans had found them, but not me, thank God.

With everything around me being blasted, I made a dash for the horses. I had to get out of there with them, and fast. I gave two sharp whistles to let them know I was coming and warn them to be ready. I untied them, and without looking around made a dash for the ditch at the back of the trees and open ground. Once over the ditch I slung the strap of my despatch bag over my head and with my bag firmly tucked under my arm I managed to get my right foot into Mabel's stirrup. We took off like lightning, with me still trying to get my left foot into Sue's stirrup. I finally managed to do it and reined the horses in close. I rode crouched between them for protection against both the British artillery fire and the German machine guns, just in case someone had their field glasses on us. I was hoping the Germans would not bother with two apparently riderless horses, and would just think they had broken free during the shelling.

We veered north-west and reached the brow of a hill. It wasn't until we started to descend the other side that I swung up on to Sue. I urged the horses on at a fast gallop and only when I felt it was safe enough and I was sure that I was back in the French and British sector, with the artillery fire dying away in the distance, did I slow down to give the horses a breather.

I kept riding in a north-westerly direction for several hours. I didn't want to get back behind enemy lines again. I could feel the horses tiring and I knew the river wasn't far away. Finally I saw it just ahead of us; the water was shimmering in the noonday sun. We had reached the river Somme.

I dismounted, ran down the bank and threw myself in, clothes and all. I had to get rid of the stench of urine which had been under my nose all morning and from which I was nearly choking.

I went back up the bank and pulled both the horses into the water, and we swam across to the other side. Mabel and Sue loved the water and they were happy to take their time swimming across.

I surveyed the whole area before letting go of the horses. I could see for miles around, except for a small clump of trees nearby, which I searched. There was no one in sight, The grass was lovely and green and the horses started to munch away happily.

Hunger was gripping at my stomach too, as I hadn't eaten since yesterday. I threw off my top clothes and laid them out to dry while I sat down and ate some dried beef and bread, washed down with a lot of water from my canteen, which I refilled immediately from the river.

After relaxing a while and having a smoke, I decided to press on. I had just finished packing up my things, getting ready to mount up, when I heard the sound of a breaking twig. I turned round, immediately dropping to the ground. There was someone or something in the trees to my right.

I got up ran doubled up towards the trees. I could see another rider, a German, who looked as if he had just arrived. He was taking out some field glasses from his saddle bag. I rushed at him, catching him by surprise. He lashed out, but he was no boxer and his blows were not heavy or effective. We grappled and he turned quickly and managed to get on top of me on the ground, but I brought my right leg up and threw him over my head. He landed a few feet away on his back, but I was up and on him before he could move.

I knew it was him or me, so I pulled out my knife and drew the blade across his throat. There was a lot of blood, but within a few seconds he was lying motionless. After relieving him of his gun, I wiped the blood off the blade of my knife. I was shaking. Then I searched the trees, just in case there were more riders, but I was satisfied that he was on his own.

A large black stallion with big eyes stood looking at me. He looked like an Arabian horse, and was about sixteen hands, a handsome devil. There was a black leather bag hanging from his saddle. I untied the bag and looked inside. There were maps, a large one of Amiens, and reports and some reconnaissance drawings, and from the drawings I could see the areas around the Somme and to the north-east: Mametz, Ovillers and Thiepval. The reports could easily be translated back at Headquarters.

I untied the stallion and waved my arms in the air to send him on his way. He galloped off, but then seemed to change his mind and stood about fifty yards away. He was eyeing Mabel and Sue and scraping the ground with his right hoof. Then he reared majestically up on his hind legs. He did not want to gallop off and be free; it seemed he wanted to be with the mares.

I took off at a gallop on Mabel, but the stallion kept pace several yards behind. I realized I could not be looking over my shoulder for the next few hours wondering where he was, so I decided to take him along. I tied him to Mabel and decided that if he gave me any trouble I would cut him loose and shoot him if necessary.

He seemed happy to gallop alongside Mabel on my right side, while Sue was on my left. We galloped along mile after mile without incident.

Thoughts kept rushing through my head. Why was the German so far west? Had he lost his way like me? Had he just ridden from Amiens? Was he doing some reconnaissance before crossing the river?

I shook my head. I had to stay alert. I searched the horizon and assured myself that I was completely alone.

The Somme valley was covered with poppies. They were so thick that it was like riding on a red carpet, not like the earlier fields I had travelled, which were only dotted with red.

It was three o'clock on a Sunday morning when I reached Company Headquarters south-west of Mametz, after taking a route to keep me clear of the enemy. I gave in my despatch bag and the German's bag. There was a look of great surprise on the Lieutenant's face when I handed it to him.

I fed and watered the horses, keeping the stallion

separated from Mabel and Sue, and after having something to eat I collapsed in the hay. For the first time in quite a while I was out of harm's way and I drifted off to sleep as soon as my head went down.

"Wake up lazybones!" I heard a voice saying. "It's seven o'clock, time to get up."

The voice sounded familiar, but it took me a while to rouse myself. "Come on Charlie boy, I've brought you breakfast." It was Ginger.

"Ginger, it's great to see you!" I said. "You're the first familiar face I've seen so far. What are you doing here?"

"Oh, I've been here for six weeks. More to the point, what are you doing here?" said Ginger.

"Oh, I'm here, there and everywhere these days. I've been running around like a blue-arsed fly. This time Friday morning I was being piddled on by the Germans near Verdun."

I told Ginger what had happened and he laughed out loud. "Well that's what you get for sleeping with the enemy" he said. But then he frowned, realising how close I had come to becoming a corpse.

"You had better be careful Charlie boy, you were very lucky to get out of there" he said. "The army ranks have grown a bit recently and there are still more joining up. There's quite a few thousand of us over here now."

"Yeah! And thousands of our lads and the French dead too" I said.

"I've been hearing about that, have they really lost that many?"

"With all that shelling down at Verdun it's a wonder there's any one left alive" I replied. "The French and the British have lost a lot of men."

Ginger turned to the stallion I had kidnapped, which was in a stall a few feet away.

"What have we got here then?" he said. "That's a handsome beast. How did you come by him? He's not one of ours, I know that." I told Ginger about the German I had met.

"Well it was either him or you, and I'm glad it was him. This one'll fetch a few guineas I wouldn't wonder."

"How much do you reckon?"

Ginger scratched his head, studying the big black horse. "I'd say upwards of a hundred guineas."

"That's a lot of money. Are you sure?"

"Yeah, he's a lot of horse. Well Charlie, if the army don't take him off you, you'll be a rich bloke when this is all over."

"You'll have to make sure the army doesn't get its hands on him Ginger, you're in charge of the horses and I'm counting on you to keep him out of sight and out of harm's way."

"And how do you think I'm going to keep this big fella hidden? The best thing you can do is take him out of here."

"Where can I put him?" I said.

"Under your backside, of course. Ride him - give Mabel and Sue a rest, which I'm sure they deserve. I'll find you another horse to match him. I think I know just the fella. You got a name for this big black stallion?"

"I was thinking of calling him Black Jack."

"Yeah. That's a good name for him."

Ginger disappeared and returned fifteen minutes later with a new mount. He brought him right up to Black Jack in the stable. The new horse was whinnying and snorting, bringing his front legs up and scraping the air. It seemed he was pleased to meet Black Jack, but I wasn't sure how Black Jack was feeling about it, although they did snort at each other and touch noses.

"He's come over from Ireland" said Ginger. "We had a shipment a while back and he's the best of the bunch. It seems I'm always giving you the best of the bunch."

"OK, I'll have to see how they get along. I think they may be all right together."

"What you going to call him?" asked Ginger.

"Well he hasn't stood still yet, so I guess I'll call him Dancer."

Dancer was a bit of a mixture; brown mostly with a black mane and tail and stood about 15 hands, not as tall as the stallion. The two horses did get along, and it was so important that they did, as my life depended more and more on the horses each day.

I was sent off early with a despatch, heading west away from the fighting towards Amiens, but well north of it, which I was very pleased about, but it wasn't long before I was sent back to Verdun.

Chapter Six

As the months passed, the run from our headquarters north of the Somme Valley to the one near Verdun became a regular run. About once a month I would also be sent up to our headquarters near Mametz.

I saw Ginger often during the winter of 1914, which was a harsh one, and we learned that in November Britain and France had declared war on Turkey. The severe winter carried on through till spring, when there was incessant rain and I was glad of my waterproof cape, which I seemed to be wearing almost every day. Some of the beautiful fields had turned to mud now.

Our boys were making some headway in the different fields of battle. They were gaining ground and moving closer to Mametz, digging more and more trenches and turning the fields into a quagmire. It was the same in the region of Ovillers and Thiepval. I had difficulty with the horses as they became bogged down, and on several occasions I had to dismount and pull them out of the mud.

Suddenly the sun shone and the earth seemed to dry out a bit. It was now May 1915. Our lads were moving up towards Thiepval. The Germans had occupied this place and dug themselves a maze of trenches the previous year. They were also well dug in at Ovillers and at Mametz.

I returned back to Mametz to find Ginger, who couldn't wait to tell me that word had gone round that the *Lusitania*, a Cunard Liner with hundreds of Americans on board, had been torpedoed by a German submarine and sunk off the south coast of Ireland.

"Those poor souls" I said. I could imagine my Dad saying the same words. I looked at Ginger and he had tears in his eyes.

"Do you know anyone who was on that ship?" I asked.

"No."

"Well what's the matter with you? You're alive and well, aren't you. The sun is shining today and you're well away from the front line."

"It's not that Charlie. I've been talking to one of your mates, Harry Jenkins. He arrived here two weeks ago and came to look at the horses. He said you and he are great pals. He has some news for you."

"Harry is here? Where is he? Trust Harry to be looking over the horses."

"I'll go and get him, while you see to your horses" said Ginger.

It had been a long time since I had seen Harry. He had changed a bit, grown up you might say. I guess we were all growing up fast now, with this war hanging over all of us. When he appeared we flung our arms around each other, and we both stood for a few moments hugging each other with tears in our eyes.

"How are you mate? How long you been in the army? Where you headed?" I threw so many questions at him all at once he didn't answer any of them, but looked at me with tears running down his cheeks.

"Hello Charlie."

"What's wrong," I said.

"It's Bert" he said.

"What's the matter with Bert? Has he got himself into trouble again?"

"No Charlie. I don't know how to tell you this, there's no easy way."

"What?"

"He went down at Gallipoli."

"What you talking about Harry? Bert's in India. I know my geography might not be the best, but I don't think that's anywhere near Turkey, you must be mistaken."

"No Charlie. His regiment was called back from India a long while ago. He was shipped first to Malta, then on the HMS *Implacable* east to Gallipoli."

"Are you sure about this?"

"Yes Charlie. I saw your mum and dad before I left last month and they had just heard the news."

It was a little while before I could take in what Harry was saying. I slumped to the ground.

"How did he die, I want to know how he died?"

"Well as far as I know they were put out in small boats and landed on a strip of beach. They had to climb a steep cliff, and it was when they went over the top of the cliff most of them got shot. The Turks were just sitting there waiting for them. Bert was shot in the chest. They got him down from the cliff, but he was in a bad way. He was shipped back to Malta, and that's where he died a short while later. Bert was buried on Malta, Charlie, they don't bring the bodies back home."

Bert dead! Our Bert! I would never see him again. Thoughts and visions of Bert came rushing into my head. I could see him chasing that bloody cockerel. I ran out of the stable and out of the camp and I kept running along the muddy road. I threw myself down by the side of the road and sobbed. I felt as if my heart had shattered into a thousand pieces.

Harry had followed me out of the camp and was tugging at my uniform.

"Charlie, I'm sorry mate, I really am, but you wouldn't have wanted me to keep this from you would you? Come on mate, let's get back to the camp, before we're missed."

He was right, of course. I was glad he had told me.

"What about Fred? Where's Fred? Has anyone heard from him?"

"Fred's OK. Your mum and dad heard from him recently and he's on the Western Front."

"So you mean to say he could be here somewhere?"

"Yes that's right. Fred didn't know exactly where he was being sent. Maybe he's somewhere in these trenches. He's been made a sergeant, your dad said."

"What else? Do you have any more news from home?"

"Yes. Mary's looking forward to see you again."

"Mary? What you talking about, she's your girlfriend?"

"Well just because I liked her didn't mean that she liked me, not in that way, you know what I mean, romantically. No Charlie, she's quite smitten by you. Matter of fact she spends most of her free time round the farm with your Mum and Dad, just waiting for you to come home. Mary is quite sweet on you Charlie. I thought you knew that?"

"No, I didn't know that Harry. Anyway, what you doing here? Are you helping Ginger with the horses?"

"No such luck Charlie, I'm a runner. I take messages from trench to trench, and with you being a rider and me a runner do you think we might help to push the Hun back to where they belong? What do you say Charlie?"

"Sure, I think we can make a difference Harry, keeping the line of communication open is very important, but it's going to take quite a few bullets to stop this lot and push the Hun back before we bring this war to an end Harry, and some very brave soldiers too. Let's do our bit, and hopefully we will be home soon. You just make sure you keep your head down when you're hopping from trench to trench, you don't want to get it blown off."

"You take care too, Charlie, I worry about you out there all alone. Don't take any chances, mate. Ginger told me about that Hun who had Black Jack. You did the right thing, you can't hesitate out here. It's kill or be killed."

1916 brought still more new recruits to the Somme, and I began to wonder whether there was anyone left at home looking after the womenfolk. I overheard some of the officers talking, and one said there were an estimated

250,000 of our soldiers in France. A million new recruits had joined up after Lord Kitchener's appeal, and quite a few thousand of them were now swelling the army on the Somme. I wondered just how many of us were going to return home.

Our armies were north of the River Somme and as the months dragged by the digging went on, with more and more trenches being dug. Everyone was getting ready for what they now called 'the big push'. I began to hate France and the Somme as it had deteriorated so much, from an expanse of pretty countryside into a muddy hell hole.

On my last visit south to our headquarters near Verdun, the French seemed to have held their position there and were managing to keep things well under control, gaining a little more ground, with the aid of the British. There was some talk that they might give us a hand with the 'Big Push' against the Hun up at Thiepval and Mametz.

In June things started to move quickly. Our guns opened fire at Mametz, Ovillers and Thiepval. There was a constant bombardment from our guns day and night and at Thiepval the sound was deafening. I was up and down the area from Thiepval to Mametz with despatches, then back again to Ovillers; our trenches stretched for more than twenty miles.

Then on the night of 30th June all became silent and still, except for lots of flares in the night sky. The orders came that the first wave of soldiers were to go over the top the next day, July 1st, at 7.30 am, and the soldiers were given an assurance that because of our heavy shelling over the past several days, resistance would be at a minimum. We all assumed that the British shells had taken their toll on the Germans and that things might not be too bad. Perhaps we could take Thiepval quite easily.

I was sent out with a despatch before dawn and was to ride south from Thiepval to Ovillers. We were dug in to the west of Ovillers. I spent the day of July 1st down there and on the 2nd I had to ride back up to Thiepval.

Things had really started to hot up and when I was still an hour's ride from Thiepval I could hear the booming noise of the shells exploding in the distance. I was unsure how much ground the British had made since the big push, and how far forward our lines would now be, but I thought that we would almost certainly have gained a lot of ground and would have taken many of the German trenches.

As I came nearer to the battlefield I looked around to try to see how far the British had progressed, but shells were raining down and exploding over the whole area, and it was difficult to know exactly where our lines were or the enemy's. I strained my eyes looking through my field glasses (I had taken them from the German at the river) and surveyed the whole dust-filled area. There were no defined battle lines. I was surprised to see that the Germans had gained a lot of ground, pushing our army right back west to where they had been a week before. Whichever way I went it seemed I would be in great danger.

As I waited there was another rapid surge forward by the Germans and I realised that I was almost trapped. I really didn't have a choice but to go round the back of the German lines. I didn't want to be sandwiched in the middle under all that gunfire. But I had found on my previous rides that the Germans didn't have a supply line behind them and I thought I might just be OK.

Then the dust cleared slightly and I could make out the German lines more clearly on my left flank. I swept around them, giving them a wide berth, and then decided to come down from the north with the Germans still on my left flank. There was fierce fighting, and where the shells were landing they were throwing up great clumps of earth and making dense dust clouds.

I pulled the horses up and quickly surveyed the whole area again. I had to ride south west, and fast, to reach our lines. I dismounted and reined Sue and Mabel close together. I arranged the horses so as to give me maximum protection from the Hun's shells, putting Sue farthest to the left of me and then Mabel, being the larger horse, next to her, and then took off, clinging to the right side of Mabel so I was putting both the horses between me and the artillery shells.

I sent the horses off at a fast gallop. Then I rolled myself up into as small a ball as possible, hanging onto the side of Mabel and trying to keep out of range of the artillery fire and get to the British lines. We had to cross a newly-established area of no man's land, and I hoped I wouldn't be spotted. The armies didn't normally fire on loose horses, so I wanted to make it look as if Sue and Mabel were riderless.

But it didn't work out that way. As I rode by close to our

trenches, the Germans turned their guns towards me. I was almost at the British trenches when Sue took a hit. Her reins were yanked out of my hands and she went down.

I swung up on Mabel and dug my heels in, trying my best to zigzag to make her a more difficult target. I could see that she had also been hit, as she was bleeding from the shoulder. We managed to get through to our lines by the skin of our teeth. But it was then difficult to pull Mabel up, as she was going full gallop and it was some distance before I could bring her to a stop.

A young private came running up to me. "I saw you come in," he said. "Are you all right?"

"Yes, but I lost one of my mounts and this one's been hit in the shoulder, can you get someone to take a look at her?"

With that the soldier ran off, but he was soon back with a medic (vets were very thin on the ground). The private went off with Mabel and the medic and I delivered my despatch.

The Colonel of the regiment shook my hand.

"We thought you weren't going to make it. Nice piece of riding that. Sorry you lost one of your horses."

"Thank you sir" I said. With that I left the Colonel to go and see if I could do something about Sue.

"Carson, are you all right?" It was Heywood walking towards me, the only other despatch rider I had seen since our training. "I was behind our lines when I heard that two horses were headed our way and when I asked what they looked like, I knew it was Mabel and Sue straight off. I was told there was no rider, but I knew you'd be tucked down in there somewhere. The Captain had his field glasses on the horses and when you popped up he was really surprised."

"What are you doing up here at Thiepval?" I said.

"Well like you, I have been bringing in despatches. I couldn't let you have all the glory!" He laughed. "I got here some time before the big push and I've been here ever since. Sorry about Sue getting hit."

"Yes, she must be lying out there" I replied. "I need to get out there as soon as I can."

"She's gone, Carson, sorry. One of the lads put her out of her misery. She was trying to get up and we couldn't see her in such agony."

We both sat down. I was sad about losing Sue and was now thoroughly exhausted. It was then that Heywood said, "Carson you've been hit! There's blood running down your boot."

I glanced down to see that a piece of shrapnel had pierced my boot.
Heywood helped me off with it. My sock was quite wet with blood, but fortunately my boot had taken most of the impact and I had only a small wound.

"I'll go and get the medic, you stay here and rest" said Heywood. He dashed off and brought the medic back. The medic found just a small piece of shrapnel near my ankle and assured me I only had a flesh wound. Mabel, on the other hand, had quite a big wound in her shoulder and would clearly be out of action for a while.

The Lieutenant came by the canteen and told me to

rest up for a couple of days to make sure there would be no infection in my ankle. Heywood was never far away, and in the morning he was again asking me whether I was all right. He had sent a private over with some new boots for me, but I told him I didn't want them as I would have no time to break them in, and said I would be grateful if he could find someone to patch up my old one, which he said he would.

Heywood came to sit with me at meal times and we started to compare notes about where we had been and what was happening out there beyond the trenches. I was surprised to hear that he hadn't been on any long runs; he had made only short trips around Thiepval. He was trying to recover from a bad fall in which he had injured his right arm, and was waiting to be transported out.

I told him it was pretty much the same throughout the Ardennes, with the Germans well dug in, and that it would be quite a task to dislodge them. I did say I was surprised that we hadn't managed to gain some ground here after all the shelling we had done before the 'Big Push'. It seemed to amount to nothing.

Heywood said we had lost so many men on July 1st that over these last few days the generals were having to rethink their strategy.

"I came round the back of the German lines and there is no resistance back there, I can't see why we can't get around them" I said. "Why are we hitting them head on? It doesn't make sense."

"Well you know the generals, you do it their way or not

at all' replied Heywood. "I overheard someone say that a battalion would head north west of Thiepval to take up a position there, that's where I have been several times. Maybe there'll be a two-pronged attack. We'll have to wait and see."

"I don't know how I'm going to get back to Mametz, with Sue gone and Mabel hurt."

"Don't worry, take my mounts, I shan't be needing them, not for a while anyway" he said.

The private returned my boot, which had been crudely patched, but someone had done their best under difficult circumstances, and as long as there was no chance of any rain getting in I was quite happy. A lot of soldiers were complaining of trench foot, having been unable to keep their feet dry, and were suffering the consequences.

"By the way, there's a letter for you Carson, it's been sitting there for quite a while waiting for you to collect it," said Heywood.

That afternoon I collected my letter; it was from Mum and Dad.

Dear Charlie,

We are still reeling from the shock of Bert's death and don't know how we are getting through the days. We can't wait until both you and Fred return home. Fred is OK, and is in Ypres, in Belgium. Mary and Ben are helping out around the farm in their spare time. We have sixteen new calves and they are all doing fine.

We both send our love, and pray that you will return home safely to us soon.

God bless you.
Love, Mum & Dad.

We had started to make some headway at last, moving forward in the trenches, and little by little we began to gain ground and we were not losing so many of our men. The lads had been able to knock out some of the Hun's machine guns, which had been picking off a lot of our lads.

It was now mid-September, and every day from the beginning of the month it had rained. With so much rain the earth became increasingly waterlogged and slippery. I had never seen so much mud. Even when we were sheltering inside and ate our food it seemed to smell and taste of mud. You could never quite get rid of it from your hands, or clear the smell of it from your nostrils.

Back at Mametz, where we had gained a lot of ground, I was leaving the camp and leading Black Jack and Dancer up a steep slippery slope when someone called out, "Do you want a hand, mate?"

"No, I can manage," I replied.

I looked up and there was Ferguson.

"Hello Carson, how you getting on?" He grabbed hold of Black Jack's reins and gave him a yank to help me get him and Dancer up the slippery slope.

Ferguson hadn't made the grade as a despatch rider, and he had been very upset at the time. I had not seen him since passing out.

"Have you seen anything of the other lads?" I asked.

"Well I heard that Adams got his horses shot from under him, and while he was making it back to Headquarters on foot, he got shot himself. Faraday copped it early on. Heywood is still around somewhere, I think."

"Yes I met up with him at Thiepval, he has had a bit of an accident and won't be riding for a while."

I started to mount up and Ferguson asked me where I was headed.

"South" I said. In fact I was going north, but I was never allowed to divulge where I was headed. "Maybe I'll see you when I get back," I said. I waved goodbye to him and cantered off. Only Harry knew where I was going, because I had told him I was 'going to see Tom' - 'T' for Thiepval, 'O' for Ovillers and 'M' for Mametz.

This was a day when I knew things would change drastically. I had gone just a few miles from the camp when I saw a British tank trundling along. I had heard about tanks, but I had never seen one before, and it was quite impressive. I could imagine the enemy fleeing the trenches at the sight of this large mechanical beast.

The horses reared up and I had to get off the muddy track to let it pass. I didn't know how many of these big machines we had, but I was very happy to see just this one. I was quite sure the Hun didn't have any, at least I hadn't seen any around in the German sector, or the French sector for that matter.

Sure enough, by the end of September we had taken

Thiepval. By November we were pushing further north, slipping and sliding our way along. The mud was indescribable. We had had only had a few dry days since the beginning of September, and now there was the added problem of fog, which became so dense at times that it was difficult for me to see where I was going. I took my bearings by keeping the sound of the artillery fire to my right, as that was the only way I could be sure that I was heading north. I couldn't read my map and I didn't want to strike a match just in case there was anyone in the area.

At times I had to dismount and walk in front of the horses, guiding them along. It reminded me of the time when I had seen a bus conductor walking in front of his bus on a foggy day when I had gone to London. The fog had descended so quickly it blanked everything out. At least the bus conductor had had a torch - I of course didn't have one, and even if I had it wouldn't be sensible to use it, as I never knew when I might bump into the Hun. I was hoping I wouldn't fall down a hole and break a leg or that the horses wouldn't get injured.

Whenever I reached higher ground and the fog became less dense, I would survey as much of the area as I could. Peering below me, I could just see the red glow of the gunfire through the dense fog.

★ ★ ★

The following spring, 1917, the Germans started to throw everything at the British and French at Verdun. The battle raged day after day, month after month, until the winter weather in November brought everything to a halt. The fields once again turned into a quagmire and all armies were bogged down and unable to move. Then finally the French and the British managed to push the Germans back.

As 1917 went on I began to see more planes in the sky, and I knew it would not be long before the war took a turn for the better. Our losses became less and with the help of the pilots' reports of the locations of the enemy trenches the Germans were soon beaten back.

I met up with Harry, still hopping from trench to trench with messages and trying to keep his head down. He told me he had run into his friend Tom Watson in one of the trenches and that Tom had heard from home that our hero Buffalo Bill had died in January. I was quite upset. What a great horseman he had been, and what a great Indian Scout; very courageous too in his younger days and very handsome.

It was difficult to imagine what was going on in other parts of the world far, far away from this war. We heard that the American soldiers had joined in the war, and were helping us to defeat the enemy. The Australian and Canadian Corps, whose troops had been busy up at Amiens, helped defeat the Germans there. Soldiers from all over the Empire and from other foreign lands were a great help to us in defeating the enemy. The war finally ended with the Armistice on 11th November 1918.

Chapter Seven

I arrived back in Britain at the beginning of December 1918. Ginger told me to wait until after dark before I left the ship with Black Jack, as although he didn't belong to the British Army, I could be stopped and asked questions and prevented from taking him away until the Army was satisfied that he didn't belong to them, and this could maybe take months. I would have to explain how I had come into possession of him and it would not be easy telling them he had belonged to the Hun and was not registered on any British paperwork.

I was hanging around near the horses when Captain Wilcox came by.

"Hello Carson, I thought I would find you here" he said. "I suppose you want to get off home as quickly as possible?"

"Yes sir, I'm just leaving." I made a move to pick up my bag and be on my way.

"I think you'll need this, Carson" he said.

"Sir?"

"You will need this." He was holding out a folded piece of paper. "You'll need this to get your horse off the ship and through the gates. It's your proof of ownership."

I couldn't believe what I was hearing. The Captain thrust the paper into my hand. He stood with his right hand outstretched and shook my hand and said, "You're a brave man Carson, good luck."

"Thank you sir, thank you!" was all I could think of to say.

Ginger was round behind the horses and he heard every word. With a beaming smile, he brought Black Jack forward and handed me his reins.

★ ★ ★

It was the early hours of the morning when I rounded the corner of the lane from Barney's field. Everything seemed changed now. I had not seen the place for over five years. The old cockerel had gone, but there was a new one crowing as I entered the yard.

I tied Black Jack to the fence, as I wasn't quite sure which field to put him in. I looked up at the house and saw Dad staring down from the window. It was as if he knew I was coming home today and was waiting for me. He disappeared and was soon flinging open the back door with Mum behind him. I ran up to them and threw my arms around them both. Tears were running down my face, and Mum and Dad were crying too. We stood for a while just hugging and kissing with Dad saying, "Thank God you're home safe and sound son, we've missed you so much."

Dad then threw a glance at Black Jack. "Who does this handsome fella belong to?" he said.

"Oh he's mine" I said. "I've brought him home to go to Ben's Dad's stud farm for breeding."

"He's a fine-looking horse" said Dad. He crossed the yard to the fence where Black Jack was tied up. All three of us were standing admiring the horse when a young woman appeared holding a small boy.

"This is Millie and her son Albert" said Mum. "She's Fred's wife, your sister-in-law. I wrote to you to say Fred had got married."

"I didn't know" I said. "I never got that letter." I turned to Millie. "Hello," I said shyly.

"Hello Charlie, I've heard a lot about you," she said, and threw her arms around me, pressing me close to her.

"Say hello to Uncle Charlie" she said to Albert.

I scooped the little boy up in my arms and gave him a big hug and a kiss. Then I saw Fred through the window and went inside to greet him. It was so many years since I had last seen him. We hugged and cried and hugged some more until little Albert ran into the kitchen and forced himself between us.

"Daddy, come and see Uncle Charlie's horse, he's so big. Can I have a ride on him Uncle Charlie? Come and see Uncle Charlie's horse Daddy!" he repeated. "He's as black as Newgate's knocker."

Fred and I burst out laughing. "How old is he?" I asked. I knew he could be no more than three and a half years old. Fred laughed out loud. "Well I thought he was three, but the things he comes out with I'm not really sure any more" he said.

All the family stood outside admiring Black Jack, but I stayed in the house looking around. It hadn't changed much, except for a new kitchen table and new chairs. I looked into the parlour and found that it had been made into a bedroom with a large double bed and a small bed. I guessed that this was now Fred, Millie's and little Albert's room.

I went upstairs to where Fred, Bert and I used to sleep and found that everything was just the same as when I had left. I opened the drawers to find Bert's stuff still there; nothing had been moved. Fred's drawers were empty, but mine were just as I had left them.

I pulled off my boots and flung myself down on the bed. It was 3 am. As soon as my head hit the pillow I was asleep.

When I awoke I wasn't sure at first whether my homecoming had been a dream. I looked around the bedroom. Sure enough, I was home. I was still in my uniform, but someone, probably Mum, had thrown a quilt over me to keep me warm. It was dark and I didn't know what time it was, but I had a faint recollection of hearing the cock crow.

I turned on the light and saw that it was 4.15. I thought it was too early to get up just in case I woke everybody in the house, but then I heard voices coming from downstairs. I washed and dressed and went downstairs to see who was up so early in the morning and saw all the family sitting round the table having tea.

"Good afternoon" said Fred. "You're still alive then."

I looked back at my watch, and I realized it was not morning but afternoon. I had slept for 13 hours.

"Why didn't you wake me?" I said.

"Mum and Dad have been up to your room several times, but you were dead to the world. I guess it's the first time you've slept more than four or five hours for quite a few years. Ben came over this morning to see you, he said he'll come back this evening."

At five thirty there was a knock at the door. Dad went to open it and I followed after him. It was Harry.

"Hello Mr Carson" he began. He was just about to say something when he saw me behind Dad.

"Charlie! Welcome home!" he cried. Dad moved to one side, and I saw to my horror that Harry's left arm was missing. I must have been staring at him in complete shock.

"Oh yeah, that" he said. "It happened in October. We were almost done out there in France and then this happened."

For a few seconds I just couldn't speak. I felt the tears welling up in my eyes. Then I grabbed hold of Harry, flinging both my arms around him. I hugged him and we both cried.

"I'm sorry mate, I'm so sorry," I said.

"Well at least I'm still alive, the other five blokes I was with in the trench weren't so lucky. We got a direct hit by a mortar shell, so I guess I'm the lucky one."

"And the war almost over, what rotten luck" I said.

"Yeah, well the lads were still being killed right up to the ceasefire as you know. It was just the last mad burst of desperation by the Hun. They didn't want to accept defeat."

We went through to the kitchen and Mum gave us some tea. There was another knock on the door, and Dad went to see who it was. A moment later he brought John, Ben and Mary into the kitchen. There were hugs and kisses all round, and Mary burst into tears as soon as she saw me. Everyone looked quite a bit older, and I saw that Mary had grown into a beautiful young woman.

We sat around the kitchen table asking each other questions and trying to fill in the five years since we had last seen each other. Harry asked me whether I had kept Black Jack and I said yes, he was out in the field. Ben, John and Mary said they were anxious to see him.

I learned that Ben's dad had offered Harry a job on his farm working with his horses, and I was pleased for him as I was wondering what he would do now that he only had one arm. I said to John that I would like his father to take Black Jack on to his farm to put him out to stud. John, Ben and Harry were very excited at the prospect of breeding their horses with Black Jack. John said he had heard a lot about him from Harry and what a magnificent stallion he was.

Dad came into the kitchen holding a torch. "Here" he said, handing it to me. "Go and show the folks Black Jack, I put him in the stable. Take some matches to light the lantern inside the door."

We put on our coats and went outside. Snow had been falling and it was now quite deep. Once inside the stable I could see Bessie. I had almost forgotten about her, but she hadn't forgotten about me. She reared up to welcome me home. I went over to her and hugged her round the neck and she threw her head up and down, as she often did when she was happy and excited.

Farther down in the stable was Black Jack. I lit another lantern near his stall so that John, Ben, Mary and Harry could all see him clearly.

"He's a beauty isn't he?" said Harry.

John and Ben stood looking Black Jack up and down. John said, "Well Harry was right, he is a magnificent horse. I don't think I've seen anything quite like him. Look how black and shiny his coat is. Look at those deep black eyes, and that head and ears. He's a great horse. If we manage to breed him what are your plans, Charlie?"

"Well, we'll have to see what he produces first and maybe with a bit of luck we might be able to get a racehorse from him, let's wait and see. Whatever happens we'll share him between us."

Harry was very happy at the prospect of looking after Black Jack and was glad to know he was going to be part of our plans and be useful in the future. At last he was getting his wish of working with horses fulfilled. I guess he had thought that at one point his life was over, but he could now see that his future had never looked so bright.

John and Ben said goodbye at the gate and asked me to say goodbye to Mum and Dad. They wouldn't come back into the house as the snow was getting worse and they had to get off home down the lane in their cart. Harry went with them, but Mary stayed back for a second to say goodbye. She hugged me and kissed me on the cheek and said with tears in her eyes that she was so glad I was back home safe and sound and that she had missed me every single day I had been gone. I felt I was seeing her for the very first time. I was very struck by how beautiful she had become.

Mary climbed into the cart and they all waved goodbye as they left. I took my boots off just inside the kitchen and banged them against the outside wall to get all the snow off. Then I shook my coat, which was white with snow. I looked out into the night and saw that we were in for a real blizzard. I hoped that John, Ben, Mary and Harry would make it back to the farm all right. I guessed that Harry would spend the night with them.

I went back in to find Fred sitting at the kitchen table. He wanted to know all about my time in the army. I told him that except for the two occasions when I found myself under heavy shell fire, once down in Verdun and then later up at Thiepval, I was pretty much OK. We chatted for hours. He told me about his time in Ypres and how in one village his regiment had had to flush out the enemy house by house, street by street.

I noticed that his breathing was laboured and asked him what was wrong. "Have you got a cold?" I asked.

"No Charlie, I was gassed up in Ypres. The Hun bombarded us with gas shells, and it's messed up my lungs. Sometimes I don't feel too bad, but other times I feel as though I can't breathe. It's like having asthma, only a lot worse. I had to leave the army early. I've been home since the spring. Most of our regiment have breathing problems and quite a few didn't make it. I guess I'm lucky to be alive. I'm not too bad in the warmer weather, but this cold air sets me off coughing."

"You will get better won't you, with a lot of rest?"

"I've been told there's nothing anyone can do, I'll just have to live with this now. I should be all right if I don't overdo things."

Neither of us mentioned Bert directly. I guess it was too painful to talk about him. His name was mentioned only once, when Fred said "Did you know that old cockerel died soon after Bert? I wonder whether he came back just to settle the score with him."

"Yes, he really hated that cockerel" I said with a smile.

"What do you think about Mary?" said Fred. "She seems quite taken by you. By all accounts she has been over here seeing Mum and Dad quite a lot while you were away. As a matter of fact she and Millie have become quite close as well. I think she's really beautiful, don't you Charlie?"

"Yeah, I guess she is" I said.

The winter was very harsh and it was almost impossible to do anything on the land. It was hard enough to try to keep the cattle alive as the temperature plummeted and we tried to keep the animals under cover as much as possible. The water in the troughs was always frozen and we were constantly trying to thaw out the ice.

Dad, Fred and I worked side by side, milking the cows and getting the hay to the cattle. All the while I kept a close eye on Fred, and as soon as he showed signs of tiring I sent him back to the house to rest. I put blankets over Bessie and Black Jack as I didn't want them to go down with a chill. We didn't see much of John, Ben and Mary during this time as I guess they had their hands full looking after their own farm and horses.

* * *

In the early months of 1919, the crocuses started to push up from the ground and the temperature began to lift a little. The snow started to melt and the cows were eager to get out into the fields. There were quite a lot of cattle now and we were glad to let them all out, as it had been very difficult trying to keep them all under cover. A few of the cows were in calf and the vet became a regular visitor. Millie and Fred were expecting their second child that August, and Millie had been told that she should be prepared to expect twins.

It was March before Ben came over to fetch Black Jack to take him to his Dad's farm. I was a bit sorry to see him go, but consoled myself knowing that he would only be a short distance away and I could always ride over to their farm on Bessie any time I liked.

I began to see a lot more of Mary, and in May I asked her whether she would consider marrying me. "I don't have to consider it" she answered, with a huge smile. "Yes, yes, yes!" She flung her arms around me and said. "Charlie, I've always loved you, since the very first time I saw you with Ben. I've been hoping for this to happen for years. In fact I think I would have died if you hadn't asked me to marry you!"

So that was decided. Both our families were very happy when we announced our engagement and our plans to marry in June. But I had made it quite clear to Mary that I wasn't sure I could settle down in England now, and that I might want to live abroad for a while. She said, "Wherever you go Charlie, I'll go with you. I can't live without you."

I had been pondering the idea of joining the Royal Canadian Mounted Police for some time. I had heard that this was a fairly new police force and they needed recruits who had good horsemanship skills. There were commissions to be had for the right people joining up early.

I was accepted straight away, and with Mary having no objections to living abroad, we made plans that as soon as we were married we would travel to Canada.

Dad was now able to get help on the farm, since all the lads were back from the army, and Fred felt a little bit better with the warmer weather. He and Millie were happy to live on the farm with Mum and Dad, and with me gone, Fred and Millie could live upstairs with their family, so Mum could have her parlour back.

I asked Fred to take charge, along with Ben, of any foals which were born from Black Jack and papers were signed to this effect, giving Fred my power of attorney to deal with things as he saw fit.

Mary and I married in June as planned, with all our

family and friends around us. Shortly afterwards we boarded a steamship for Canada. Our first stop would be Halifax, Nova Scotia, and from there we would go to Montreal, then Ottawa and then on up to Hudson Bay to start our new life. I just couldn't wait to get my scarlet jacket and my wide-brimmed felt brown hat. I just hoped they would give me a horse that was half as good as Black Jack.

THE END

ND - #0517 - 270225 - C0 - 203/127/10 - PB - 9781861511157 - Matt Lamination